Cocky Catcher

A Single Dad Sports Billionaire Romance

Cocky Billionaire Boys
Book 1

Chiquita Dennie

304 Publishing Company

Latest Releases

Series

Struck in Love

The Early Years-A Prequel Short Story
Ruthless:Antonio and Sabrina Book 1
Savage: Antonio and Sabrina Book 2
Beast: Antonio and Sabrina Book 3
Captivated By His Love:Janice and Carlo
Brutal: Antonio and Sabrina Booke 4
Redemption: Antonio and Sabrina Book 5

Heart of Stone

Broken, Book 1 (Emery & Jackson)
A Valentine's Day Short Book 1.5 Emery & Jackson
Rebirth, Book 2 (Jordan and Damon)
Reveal, Book 3 (Angela and Brent)
Bottoms Up Book 3.5 Jessica and Joseph Short
Renew, Book 4 (Jessica and Joseph)

Cocky Billionaire Boys

Cocky Catcher (Cocky Billionaire Boys Book 1)
Bossy Billionaire (Cocky Billionaire Boys Book 2)

The Fuertes Cartel
Stolen (The Fuertes Cartel Book 1)
Saved (The Fuertes Cartel Book 2)
Betrayed (The Fuertes Cartel Book 3)
Carrington Cartel
Torn: The Carrington Cartel Book 1
Claim: The Carrington Cartel Book 2
Something
Something Gained: A Romantic Comedy Book 1
Something Earned: A Romantic Comedy Book 2

Pierce Motors
Refuel: (Pierce Motors Book l)
Pressure: Pierce Motors Book 2)
Summer Break
Summer Nights: (Summer Break Book 1)
TN Seal Security
Aydin: Book 1
Nasir: Book 2
Nicco: Book 3

Standalones
Until Serena(HEA World Novel)
Temptation
She's All I Need
I Deserve His Love
Mutual Agreement
Scoring with Sadie
Exposed (A Bodyguard Novel)
Love Shorts:A Collection of Short Stories
Red Light District(A Fantasy Romance Short)

Author Note

Cocky Catcher is a standalone story originally inspired by Vi Keeland and Penelope Ward's (Stuck Up Suit). It is revised and published without the Cocky Hero brand.

This book is dedicated to my family, especially Rhonda Dennie, Grandma, and Aunt Marcia for always believing in me. Also, I want to shout out my big brother Brent Dennie, JD, Christopher, Lil James, Jazzypoo, my sisters, and best friends from Memphis. Also to all my LA besties for always supporting me. Shout out to all of my nieces, and nephews.

Disclaimer

This work of fiction contains strong language and explicit sexual content and is only intended for mature readers. This story may contain unconventional situations, language, and sexual encounters that may offend some readers. If you are looking for sweet, fluffy romance, I would recommend another book. This book is for mature readers (18+).

Author Inspiration

"Never allow anyone to steal your joy. It doesn't matter how many times someone says you can't do something. Invest in yourself—even if it's just writing down what your goals and plans are. Starting small can lead to bigger things."

—Chiquita Dennie

Introduction

I know you are ready to delve deep into this book. I'm beyond excited for you to read it and so thankful that you've chosen one of my books as one of your favorites to include on your shelf. Grab some wine and get ready for Gage and Nina in Cocky Catcher.

Character Interview: Gage Young

The infamous Gage Young, billionaire catcher of the New York Raptors and playboy, father of Tailynn Young, son of Tobias and Deborah Young. Gage can be a little arrogant, rude, and cocky. We can't be held responsible for his actions in this interview (or in the book.

Interviewer: "What do you think of being our third guest on?"

Gage: "Personally, I think I should have been your first."

Interviewer: "Cocky right out of the gate aren't you?"

Gage: "You call it cocky, I say I'm just being brutally honest."

Interviewer: "When did you first pick up a baseball?"

Gage: "When I was kid I was obsessed with watching old clips of Babe Ruth and Joshua Gibson. Two world famous baseball players."

Interviewer: "I hear you're called *A Billionaire Catcher,* is that true?"

Gage: "The media takes the smallest kernel of information and runs with it, my family has money, and I have worked extremely hard for my endorsements and salary. That's all I'll say about that."

Interviewer: "Was it love at first sight with Nina?"

Gage: "You'll have to ask her."

Interviewer: "I understand you're good friends with the founder of Pierce Motors, Jackson Pierce. How'd you two meet?"

Gage: "We met through one of our mutual friends Genesis Maguire at a charity fundraiser that he has every year. When I got in this business I wanted to make sure I gave back in any way I could and he's done great things with his investments and charity work. I admire his determination to keep his privacy and family safety a priority. They are happily married with kids. I've come to rely on them for advice a lot more as I get older and want to focus on settling down."

Interviewer: "Are you excited about the game this year?"

Gage: "Yes, I can't wait to get back out on the field."

Interviewer: "Can you give us one spoiler for something we might see?"

Gage: "Nope."

Interviewer: "Tell us your favorite vacation spot."

Gage: "My family's island in Fiji."

Interviewer: "I know I speak for all the readers today when I say that we appreciate you for stopping by and hanging out with us today.

Readers we hope you enjoy Cocky Catcher and let us know how Gage and Nina fair in this new release."

Synopsis

Can this billionaire baseball player catch more than just the World Series?

Gage Young is used to getting his way. As the hottest player in the league, this billionaire catcher is leading his team to the World Series. To make his fans swoon even more, he's a single dad that's not afraid to show off how much he adores his daughter.

Enter Nina Mitchell. As a little league softball coach, and helping out with the family business, Nina knows when its time be stubborn and how to deal with pressure, especially now that her family is being forced to sell out to make room for another strip mall. But she's not used to dealing with arrogant baseball players used to running the show.

She adores Gage's daughter but when it comes to Gage, despise is an understatement about how she feels about this cocky single dad. They're at odds about almost anything, except the attraction they can't seem to ignore.

Can Gage and Nina set their differences aside, or will

rules and regulations get in the way of what could be the love of a lifetime?

Enjoy this single dad sports romance that hits all the sweet spots with secrets, seduction, and of course a home run or two.

Chapter One

Gage

Thursday Night

New York was beautiful at this time of night. The lights of the city were twinkling like stars as I sat inside of the famous Barbetta Italian restaurant having a late dinner date. This has been the most boring date I've ever been on, and with the amount of dating I've done since I was sixteen, that's saying something. Thinking back to that time, I had a date with Tabitha where she pulled out her photos of her wedding vision board along with before and after photos of the surgery she wanted to get on her breasts and ass as a wedding gift, yeah this date makes that one look like a dream date. The live entertainment over in the corner played a version of Adele's "Hello", and all I could think about was texting my boy, Talbot, to call my phone as a rescue ring and get me out of this sham of a date. He told me not to go, but Elizabeth had hounded me incessantly over the past few weeks. So, I eventually broke down and agreed since we ran in the same circles. Sneaking a glance down at my watch, I took a sip of water wondering when this night would end. I'd pretty much come to the conclusion this wasn't going any further than a hook-up. I wasn't looking for anything long term, and besides all of my attention was focused on my daughter, Tailynn, and she wasn't afraid to let you know in a heartbeat that she wasn't sharing her daddy unless you were something special. The waiter came over and grabbed our plates. I picked up my napkin wiping my mouth, smiling as she droned on and on about her new house in the Cayman Islands as I paid the check. "How about cocktails at my place?" I asked, squeezing her in close and wrapping my jacket around her shoulders. Tailynn was with her grandparents tonight, so we'd have the place to ourselves. Normally I wouldn't have sleepovers if my daughter was home, it was out of respect, unless I was serious about someone. Leading her out of the door, I was hoping the paparazzi wouldn't be lurking outside. The last thing I wanted was to be linked to Elizabeth in the media circus. She would more than likely go along with things and make it seem like we were already engaged and expecting a bundle of joy by the morning.

We'd decided to meet up there because I had an early practice today. Spending my time listening to a woman trying to seduce me into making her my number one girl. Now, don't get me wrong; Elizabeth was a nice girl (when she wanted to be), but she was a two-time divorcee. She didn't work, and it seemed like all of her goals in life revolved around shopping and vacationing, and she could be money-hungry to an extent. If I was being honest, I wasn't even really attracted to Elizabeth. She was more of the high-society, plastic surgery, looking-good-on-your-arm-but-containing-no-substance, type of chick. In other words, somebody my parents would have loved for me to bring home and take to parties, but I wasn't going that route. I'd decided a long time ago to follow my own path in life. I wasn't looking for commitment; I was more interested in having fun while I was still young.

I opened the door right when the flash of a camera almost blinded us. Somehow, attention had grown in the media over the years as I commanded more attention in baseball. It probably had something to do with the type of women I dated or took to bed.

"Do you mind stepping to the right? My better side is on the left," Elizabeth stated, posing for the photographers. I can't believe she actually had the nerve to ask me to move to her better side for photos.

"All right, guys, that's enough. Time for me to finish my date," I said.

"Well, I was thinking that we could have a late-night conversation at my place," she said, running her hand suggestively across my chest.

"That's what I like to hear."

"You just signed a hundred-million-dollar endorsement deal with Vantage Energy Drink Company, right?" Elizabeth probed.

I could feel a headache coming on already knowing where she's taking this question. I knew I needed to shut down this interrogation immediately. I didn't think that on our first date, she'd bring up the subject of how much money I make, seeing as how she'd just divorced her second husband and received a substantial divorce settlement. She must be running out of liquid assets already. "I will not discuss money on the first date," I said bluntly.

She must have felt the vibe was off in her comment because she tried changing the subject to us going out again as we continued walking out of the restaurant.

I continued walking down the street, when suddenly another paparazzi jumped out of the alleyway and we both jerked back, completely shocked at the lengths they would go to just to get the so-called perfect shot. We suddenly bumped into another person attempting to juggle a small bag of groceries, her cell phone, and I watched as a drink fell on the ground.

"Oh shit!" the young lady screamed. Right as she bent down, I followed suit to help clean up the mess. Her features were intoxicating, even with the light glare of the camera flash, and seeing spots from the flash. She couldn't have been over five foot six or five foot seven. Our hands grazed over picking up her keys. Just then, an electric pulse thrummed through my body and caused us both to pull back. She was smiling and thanking me profusely until she looked up and met my gaze.

"Wait, it's you!" she replied, jumping back in shock.

"Yeah, I get fans at random times recognizing me and wanting an autograph and a picture, but I'm on a date, so I'll have to decline, I hope you can understand."

"Trust me, the last thing I want from you is an autograph," she scoffed, rolling her eyes.

"Oh, my God! You ruined my dress!" Elizabeth shouted, wiping her hands down her dress to try to slough off the frozen concoction that had spilled all down her front.

"What's that supposed to mean?" I asked.

"My cell phone might be broken," the young lady replied, bending down, and cursing under her breath.

I reached over and picked up her torn grocery bag to put her things on the ground that scattered away when I suddenly noticed a vibrator sitting next to her pint of Chunky Monkey ice cream.

"Looks like you're planning on having an eventful night tonight," I said, not bothering to hide my smirk.

"Give me that back," she spat as she grabbed the vibrator from me and threw it back in her bag. I could see the flush climbing up her neck, making me wonder what she looked like when she climaxed during sex.

"What's the rush?"

"If you focused more on your posture, and listening to your coach, rather than being selfish and doing your own thing, and less on what I have in my bag, you'd be hitting your stats," the sassy woman snapped, giving me a rundown on what I needed to improve on.

"Oh, you're one of those."

She reached out and grabbed her keys, picking up the torn bag.

"One of what?"

"A baseball fanatic that thinks they know the game better than the professionals. It's cute, babydoll, but I'm good over here."

She chortled in laughter. "The last World Series the Washington Nationals won, Stephen Strasburg was named MVP. The Nationals extended their lead to 6–2 in the ninth inning, with two runs scoring on a one-out single by Eaton with the bases loaded. And my girl, Simone Biles, a Houston native and Olympic gold medalist, threw out the first pitch in the second game. You know that black girl magic reigns supreme." She spoke eagerly, with a sarcastic undertone.

I could only smile. "So, you do know a little something about baseball," I said stepping in further to close the gap between us.

"Gage!" Elizabeth screamed in a choked voice.

"One second."

A loud horn blaring from a speeding car interrupted the verbal standoff between us.

She dipped her eyes low and checked her cell phone for any damage. "Casanova, you need to focus on the bimbo next to you, it looks like she is about to go nuclear on you any minute," she said as she nodded over to Elizabeth.

I chuckled at her response, looking over my shoulder at Elizabeth, who was still diligently attempting to clean the red stain off her dress with my jacket sleeve.

A cool, sweet smell like roses floated through the air. Excitement raced through me like a bolt of lightning. The woman had lush, sweeping eyelashes under that hard glare; she had pouty lips, straight white teeth, and pink, glossy lipstick. Her hair was swept into a messy bun atop her head. Her tight pajama pants hugged her petite frame, showing off her tantalizing curves. She shouldn't be using a vibrator to get off, not when there were guys like me with perfectly good hands, among other appendages, that could satisfy her needs. Did she think she couldn't find someone that was able to please her? Did someone make her lose faith and force her to use a vibrator? I was thinking way too hard about this woman in front of me. I had to just shake it off and get back to this date.

But Elizabeth was still throwing a fit and the commotion was drawing a bigger crowd. Fans and photographers were taking pictures and video, and probably livestreaming on their favorite social media platforms. The whole thing made me nauseous.

I helped the woman finish packing up and watched as she glared at both of us before limping away out to the parking lot, messing with her phone like she was trying to get it to turn on. She disappeared around the corner and I turned my attention back to Elizabeth and the crowd of onlookers. "Okay, guys, back up. I'm on a date, it's nothing serious." I was ready to finish the night early and get home to my bed.

Elizabeth groaned, stomping her feet, and walking off to the car, acting like a child that didn't get her way. Tailynn didn't even act this way when she didn't get her way with staying up late, or hanging out with her friends before getting her homework done. Shrugging my shoulders, I figured I wasn't going to get any after the money question. I saw date one was a strike out. So, I headed home to see who else I could call up.

****

Saturday morning

The gym kept the weight room up to date with the newest setup. I liked the Olympic bench because of all the points it targeted, everything from toning my shoulder muscles, to strengthening my back muscles and upper chest.

I did my normal workout chant... "Press, press, press, Gage don't need more press. Kill 'em all; put them pitchers to rest. Strike out —oops, sorry, babydoll." I apologized for bumping into the sexy beauty behind me.

"Yeah, watch where you're going," she mumbled, walking toward the mirror in front of the free weights. She dropped her towel and picked up her water bottle.

I chuckled to myself. "You may want to spread your legs wider."

"Excuse me?" she asked, looking over her shoulder, clearly appalled at my comment.

"If you're trying to get a better lock on your upper muscles with the ten-pound weights, I suggest spreading your legs wider and bending at a ten-degree angle to reap the most benefits from the workout," I explained, licking my lips, and placing the dumbbells back on the bench.

"I didn't ask for your opinion, focus on that arm of yours instead of me," she said, breathing out harshly, and resting a hand sassily on her hip.

Oh shit. I recognized that snark and that beautiful face filled with attitude. It was the girl from the other night. I liked a woman with sass and an extensive knowledge of baseball. A look of annoyance spread across her face as she recognized me too. That's crazy, it must be a small world. "Hey. It's you. How did things work out for you?"

Beads of sweat rolled down her chest but she was still hot. The exertion she was putting forth in her workout made her beautiful and glowing. As she placed the weights down and picked up her towel to wipe the sweat away, she snorted in annoyance and took a sip of water. "Your girlfriend owes me a new phone."

"I wasn't talking about the girl. I was talking about your new toy," I explained.

She tucked a lock of hair behind her ear, rolling her eyes. "You should be concerned with your girlfriend and not with what I do with my toys, Mr. Billionaire Catcher," she spat, bending down, and tying her shoelace.

Standing in front of her with my arms crossed over my chest, I asked, "How did you become such a baseball expert?" A few guys walked inside the room and their eyes were immediately drawn to her ass sitting nice and perky in her workout shorts, uncaring if she was my girlfriend or wife. My eyes were hard and filled with dislike.

They got the hint and kept moving over to the shoulder press machines. She cleared her throat, pulling me out of my standoff.

"I played a few years professionally with the U.S. Women's Softball League," she answered.

"Maybe one day you can give me a few lessons." I was teasing her, I found myself completely amused with the situation. Softball wasn't as complicated as baseball in my opinion. She must have had it way easier compared to the amount of pressure major baseball players have to go through, what with the media and diehard fans that wanted to critique every little step both on and off the field. She bent down picking up another weight, shaking her head in amusement.

"You might be cute in that Chris Evans kind of way, you know that all the girls fall in love with the guy next door type. But, you can't afford me."

I chuckled at her comment and watched her walk away from me as her ass jiggled in the tight spandex shorts. "And on that note, it's time for me to go," I said to myself, turning to head toward the showers to get dressed before practice. *Billionaire Catcher* wasn't a name I came up with myself, but it stuck just the same. All through high school and into college I played baseball. My love of baseball started while watching earlier players like Babe Ruth and Joshua Gibson. Then my older brother and cousins started to play the game. Somehow, I stuck with the game and they all went into the family business. After graduating from college, I went pro and that's when the moniker got thrown at me because of my family's legacy. The amount of time I spent playing the game, and the numerous endorsement deals combined from Nike, Gatorade, Chex cereal, and partnership with Netflix to stream exclusive baseball content with my view on the latest sports news – none of that seemed to matter somehow.

I turned the water off and stepped out of the shower, grabbing a towel off the counter in the personal bathroom for celebrities and VIP members. I was a longtime client of this establishment. As an athlete, I needed a place to work out without being hounded. This was a private gym that only VIPs and celebrities attended. Genesis Maguire, one of my friends, a billionaire CEO of a sports agency, turned me on to this place. And it had been my favorite ever since Genesis told me about the level of discretion they provided for their customers. The TV in the corner was on ESPN with the latest game playing. Chicago Tigers vs. Boston Scorpions was in the second inning with two men on base. Today wasn't a big game so I wasn't worried about either of these teams making it to Nationals, whoever won today would go up against the Utah Giants and then I needed to keep an eye on things because we would be up against the winner once we won our next game. I turned the volume up and listened to Stephen Hampton go off once again.

"Listen, this team needs their own version of a '*Billionaire Catcher*.' Obviously, they're not paying and recruiting the right people, because this game is underwhelming and lazy on both sides. I'm not seeing the results."

I shook my head, groaning. Running the towel over my hair, and dropping the towel in the hamper, I quickly pulled on a fresh pair of jogging pants and t-shirt. It never seemed to fail that my salary was mentioned in any given conversation with a sports announcer. My contract was renewed two years ago for fifty million, to be paid out over the next ten years. I promised Li'l Bit that I'd retire before I hurt myself and couldn't be around to take her to the park, movies, shopping, or playing games in the stadium field like we used to do when she was younger. I was already thirty-one, which was getting up there in professional baseball. I wanted to start a real family of my own, especially seeing as how my ex-girl-friend was about to get married. Sometimes, I was envious of her relationship—especially when I saw our daughter understanding what a healthy couple should look like. Don't get me wrong, Samantha and I got along great, and our relationship didn't end because of a scandal.

We were college sweethearts, and dated through the first two seasons of me playing pro. About five years ago, we'd decided it was best to be just friends. My career was taking up more and more of my life and I was traveling all the time. She wanted a guy that could commit, and who would not get caught up in this celebrity lifestyle.

Pushing through the back door of the gym, I was immediately bombarded with flashing lights and paparazzi screaming my name. No one tells you about this part of the lifestyle when you sign your contract and become famous. Everyone always had their nose in my business.

I shielded my eyes as much as possible as I tried to barge through the crowd of fans and photographers.

"Gage! Gage! What do you think about your chances for a World Series bid this year?" the nosy reporter screamed. One girl in front of me asked for an autograph right when a reporter pushed a microphone in my face.

"Gage Young, we hear the new contract contains a morals clause with how you conduct yourself on and off the field. Is this true?" the reporter questioned pointing the microphone in my face.

"No comment, Tracey, you know better than that. Stick to the real facts, and how the team is lacking a strong outfielder and pitcher," I insisted, trying to move from in front of the door that was suddenly pushed open fast. I tripped and fell on top of Tracey as she was holding the mic in front of me just as the paparazzi took another picture of me falling on my ass. Our hands rested on the pavement before I completely fell down. "What the fuck? Watch where you're—" I yelled out, stopping myself before going any further, glancing around at the amount of people who were surrounding us, and then realizing that vibrator girl would probably get the brunt of cameras following her after this incident. I helped Tracey up, checking to make sure she didn't have any bumps or bruises as I stood up, wiping the dirt off my hands.

"Are you alright?" I asked Tracey.

"Yeah, didn't think I would become the story this time though," Tracey said giggling, motioning to her cameraman to pack up.

"Welcome to my world," I replied wryly, and left the chaos behind before even more drama could start. Turning around, I unlocked my car and dropped my gym bag in the trunk. I jumped in the driver's side turning the radio on right when Cardi B's song "Press" started back up again. Placing my shades on, I pulled out into the turning lane. I glanced in my rearview mirror and saw my new baseball friend talking on the phone animatedly. She honked at me for taking too long, and I grinned, shaking my head, as I merged into traffic.

Chapter Two

Gage

Opening the door of my condo, I heard laughter coming from the dining room. Those voices always brightened my day when everything else had gone to shit, whether it was because our team had lost, or my parents had tried to pawn me off on another female friend of the family.

I had the entire penthouse to myself, with an indoor pool, my own elevator, and a garage for my cars. I bought this place about two years ago, seeing as I knew I was not going to be settling down anytime soon. The ceilings were open, shining hardwood floors graced a large open space furnished as a combination living and dining area. My favorite colors, black and grey, flowed throughout the place, except in Tailynn's purple and gold Princess Tiana themed room. The security aspect was another factor for me having this place. As the middle son of Tobias and Deborah Young, I had the pleasure of not sticking to the norm of working for the Young family's business dynasty in the land of corporate America.

Tailynn, my sweet daughter, was eight going on

thirty. She took after her mother more than me, with her oval-shaped eyes, deep dimples on both cheeks, and dark-brown, curly hair that I was finally able to correctly put in a ponytail and barrettes that matched her outfits. Her looks matched her mom's, however her personality was all me. She was all mouth and could trash talk with the best of them.

She sat on top of the dining room table, not caring about getting any scratches on the wood from her colored pencils. Her mother hovered over her, mumbling at her to stay in the lines.

Samantha Randall was and will always be my best friend. We met in college. She was a cheerleader, and I was a jock playboy who didn't want to fall in love and lose my shot at the majors. She had a bronze complexion, oval-shaped eyes, a pointy nose, and high cheekbones, all of which Tailynn inherited. At first, I wouldn't date her because she was so short compared to the women I normally dated; they were all leggy model types. Some-how, Samantha tore those walls down, and we ended up dating for three years.

Right before graduation, she became pregnant. We had already been growing apart, my career was taking off and she wasn't into being the wife of a professional athlete. It took us a few years to smooth out our co-parenting arrangement, but after a while, Tailynn became our priority and Samantha became one of my best friends, next to my older brother Daniel. I'd even introduced her to her now-fiancé, Jason Combs, a local business owner who had a clothing store next to the tattoo shop that was owned by Talbot, another friend of mine.

"Hi, Daddy!" Tailynn jumped down off the table and ran into my arms. Rubbing her soft curls that were currently in two ponytails that her mom handled expertly, I continually marveled at her skills. She always complained about me when I helped her with her hair, because it stayed sticking up on top of her head.

"Li'l Bit!" I kissed the top of her head, as she hugged me around my neck. "How was your day, baby?" I let her go and she sat back down on the table, following the sound of Samantha's voice coming from the kitchen.

"Eat Tailynn." Samantha was cleaning the dishes in the sink as she cooked. I was planning on ordering a pizza, but since there were leftovers, I'd jump into that.

"It was good—except Momma's making me eat Brussels sprouts," Tailynn whispered in my ear.

"Tai, it won't work. You can't play your father and me against each other, we learned your ways years ago, sweetie," Samantha joked with a grin of infinite amusement lighting up her face.

"Li'l Bit, the only way to grow strong is to eat your vegetables," I responded, kissing her forehead, hugging Samantha with one arm. I respected her relationship and made sure it didn't come off as inappropriate when her fiancé was around. I grabbed a cookie off the tray that held Tailynn's snacks for afterschool, and leaned up against the counter.

"How was your day, Sam?"

Samantha stopped cutting the tomato, wiping her hands with the paper napkin. "Fine, I had some papers to grade and getting things together for Tailynn's softball game. So that was fun."

"That's cool, did you have a good day at school, Li'l Bit?" She had her mouth pinched in thought, tapping the tip of her chin thoughtfully with her finger.

"It was good, Daddy. Most of the girls on my softball

team are in my class," Tailynn answered, turning to me, her face lighting up as she spoke.

"What softball team?" I looked at her mother. "You put her on a softball team?"

Tailynn walked back to her seat as we followed behind her and I grabbed a green colored pencil and turned to help Tailynn color her picture.

She nodded with a smirk.

"You're on a softball team? I'm hurt, Li'l Bit. Why didn't you ask me to coach your team?" I tugged my sports jacket off and hugged her, sitting next to her. How cool was that? My kid's playing softball. I can't wait to teach her everything I know. Man, this is the life.

"Daddy, you're too busy to coach. Plus, I don't need any of the women falling all over you."

"Girl, yo' Daddy can't help that he's fine," I joked.

Her eyes popped wide at my impression of her mom and friends.

Samantha and Tailynn let out a peal of hysterical laughter. A lopsided grin quirked my mouth up into a smile.

"The coach she has is experienced, and she's really nice. So, don't go down there trying to take over and being all big-time, arrogant, World Series catcher. Tailynn is the star on the field. So, keep all your opinions under wraps when you take her to practice," Samantha warned me with a wink. I waved off her comment.

"How are the wedding plans going?" I questioned, quickly changing subjects, not paying attention to her little warning. Whoever this coach was I'd be the judge of if they're good or not. "Plans are good. Jason is at the shop right now, going over some last minute paperwork. We have dinner plans tonight, which is the reason why I brought Li'l Bit over to ask if you could take her to school and practice on Monday."

"You don't have to ask. Have fun at dinner and tell Jason I said what's up," I answered, kissing the top of Tailynn's head, enjoying hanging out before she got too grown and forgot about her daddy. A little later, I walked her out to the brand new Range Rover that Jason had given her for her birthday. Uh-oh, I could tell that she had that old disapproving face on.

"Saw your little interview, maybe you should try turning down the cocky I-know-everything attitude before someone hurts your feelings, Gage," Samantha scolded, turning the key in the ignition.

"Weren't you the one who told me in college to have more confidence in myself when I was out on the field? Can't help that it transferred into my everyday life. It's not like I said anything false about the team. I want another championship ring, and the only way to get to that level is by putting the best team possible around me." I shoved my hands in my pockets, shrugging my shoulders.

Samantha opened and then closed her mouth, sighing. She shrugged, putting the car in reverse, and backing up as I waved goodbye.

Chapter Three

Nina

Why am I always attracted to men that annoy me with this whole self-assured, know what you want, and I'll challenge you on everything cocky bastard attitude? He was so damn tall, like six feet or six two even, I didn't even remember. Our first meeting we literally bumped into each other, and I was looking a hot mess. *Just like right now.* "Something must be in the air for me to always look unkempt when we ran into each other," I muttered out loud. A few minutes later, I pulled into my parking space under my condo building, turning the car off and grabbing my purse to head inside. I stopped doing the dating thing after I broke up with my ex because he belittled my career ambitions, and his close-minded thinking that women shouldn't be in professional sports. I refused to limit myself for any man and I've been single for about a year now. I was about five seven with long thick hair; often my momma would say it's kinky thick. It's the bloodline of our ancestors. Being into sports I was always able to keep my figure slim, but I was still thick and curvy. All my siblings and I had a deep rich brown skin tone that we took after our mother. From my time playing softball, I've had to stay on top of getting manicures because of having calloused hands from all the time playing. Which everyone got on to me about, always making a big deal out of it. One thing I loved about myself was the dimple on my chin and lush full lips. "Ugh! Celebrity jocks are ridiculous." Getting out of the car, I walked toward the mailboxes and scowled, looking at another notice from the bank regarding an overdue payment on our mortgage for the community center. Mitchell Family Center is a place that has been in my family's life for years. Turning the key in my door, I flicked through each bill, wondering when we would ever be able to have our heads above water.

I dropped the keys and the mail down on my new, brown, wicker coffee table that I'd ordered online from my best friend's cousin's new thrift store. Maya's cousin had started and stopped so many different careers that she couldn't keep up with her. So, she'd asked if I could help support her and spread the word. Recently, I'd ordered a few pieces for my place and the community center.

Turning on the TV, I saw another reporter commenting and asking Gage Young about being this sex symbol, a playboy that can't keep it in his pants.

I sucked my teeth, still scowling. "Asshole." My phone rang with my sister Nicole's name flashing across the screen. I picked it up and swiped to answer her call. "Hey, sis, what's up?" I stretched my arms up over my head to fight the stiffness that was starting to creep throughout my body after my workout, and then made my way over to the fridge.

"Hello! What are you doing?"

Opening the door, I grabbed a fruit platter and a salad

that I'd premade last night. "Nothing. Just got home from working out, I'm exhausted and annoyed. What about you?" I replied, grabbing a knife from the drawer and a plate out of my cabinet.

"What has you all annoyed?" Nicole questioned, walking through my front door as I hung up my phone rolling my eyes at her smiling, since she just stopped by without warning.

Nicole was my younger sister at twenty-two, to my twenty-eight. She was the complete opposite of me, with her long dreads and a piercing in her lip and nose. She was on her earthy, bohemian, I'm-not-my-hair, India Arie lifestyle. Last month, she was going through a hot-girl, summer phase, wearing next to nothing, going out all the time, and dating different guys—which wouldn't have been a problem if she still didn't live at home with my parents. Even before that, she was trying to travel around the world after dropping out of college. It was a running joke in the family that we never knew who we'd get when she walked into the house.

Then, there was my older brother, Nicholas Jr., who was the best big brother a girl could ask for and had been her protector growing up. He was two years older than me, and we kind of had the same mindset with our little sister. She was spoiled and never had to work for anything. Our parents hadn't been expecting a new addition once they rekindled after a brief separation. She was the "oops" baby, so it was better to give in to her demands rather than to chastise any of her faults.

As the middle child of Nicholas Sr. and Natalia Mitchell, I had the responsibility of going to school, getting good grades, making the honor roll, taking care of my sister, going to college, and always being the good girl that everyone could count on. Sometimes, that role took a toll on me—especially when it came to men, particularly my ex. He thought that he could run all over me. I scowled remembering back on the times he wanted me to cancel my endorsement opportunities, because the attention it would bring about, or his jealousy when fans would come to games and want pictures. All he cared about was me following him around and catering to him like I was his damn momma or something.

Nicole came up behind me, stealing a grape off my plate, and I nudged her in the shoulder to get her to grab a plate for herself. "Haven't we had this conversation before about you just dropping in unannounced?" I asked.

She waved me off, making a plate of fruit and salad for herself. Seeing her jump on top of my counter that I just had repainted annoyed me even further.

"What are you doing here?"

Nicole blew out a breath of frustration, shrugging her shoulders. I could tell something was wrong. "Have you talked to Dad yet, or Grandpa?" Nicole inquired, narrowing her dark brown eyes.

"Nope, but I saw the bill from the bank today, so he'll probably be calling me soon." I moved around her, strolling to my bedroom upstairs to change clothes. My condo was on the third floor, in a gated building with security. I had two levels, with a wide balcony, patio furniture, and a small garden. My garden brought me calm and patience whenever I was upset or frustrated. It made me think of gardening with my grandmother, which was among some of my earliest memories.

Nicole tagged along behind me, eating her food, plopping down on my bed kicking up her feet, and turning on the TV. I grabbed a t-shirt and shorts out of the closet.

"Damn, he's looking like a whole snack," Nicole blurted out. I turned to look at whom she was talking about and once again, Gage Young was on my TV screen.

"Girl, please. He's the type you stay away from. He's nothing but a living and breathing heartbreak for any woman. Better off sticking to the no job, video game playing dates you're used to, sweetie."

A devilish grin played at the corners of her lips.

"Someone sounds jealous," Nicole snipped, making a goofy face, crossing her arms and legs.

"I saw him at the gym and he's literally like you see him on TV, a stuck-up jerk, all into himself," I told her.

"Really? Maybe I should go with you next time. He probably needs a strong woman."

"Nicole, your so-called workout is eating kale while looking at old Jane Fonda workout videos. You're the last person I would take to the gym." Snatching the remote out of her hands, I changed the channel before heading into the bathroom and locking the door.

"What position does he play in baseball?" Nicole shouted through the door as I turned the shower on.

I yanked the door open right as she was about to knock. "No!" I yelled pointing a finger in her face, shaking my head.

"Why are you intent on keeping me from my possible soul mate?"

"Nicole, the last thing you need is to add another man to your belt. What happened with Jeremy the professor? Or Thomas, the lead singer in that little band you were in for a few months? Oooh... or Mike, the so-called 'banker' who was really just a telemarketer for credit card companies?"

"Nina, you wound me with your words," Nicole said softly with a hand clasped over her heart.

"He's not your type. Anyway, I have my second game as the coach with my little league team soon. I'm super excited to see the girls again."

Nicole jumped up, walking into my closet, thinking she was going to steal another outfit.

Keeping the door half open, I ran into the shower.

I washed up quickly and got out before she could make off with any of my clothes.

"What time is practice tomorrow? I might come through; it's been a while since I've seen you on the field. Do you miss playing the game?" Nicole asked, holding a dress up to her body in front of my mirror. She pointed to me, silently asking if she could borrow it—even though her closet was comprised of half of my clothes already.

"You're not invited." I snatched the dress out of her hands and put it back in my closet.

"That would look cute on me. Please, can I borrow it for my date?"

"No, now get out of my bedroom. We need to figure out a plan for the center."

"When's the last time you've gone on a date? I feel a little sexual frustration all up in here." Nicole motioned her hand from the top of my chest down to my vagina. I smacked her hand away, stomping over to sit on the lounge chair.

"My love life is none of your business. Besides, taking love advice from you is not a part of my plan," I remarked right when my door swung open.

My best friend, Maya, strutted inside, wearing her usual oversized Joan Crawford shades, six-inch heels, and size-six Stella McCarthy dress. She loved throwing labels around.

"I have arrived. Please, no pictures—unless it's of my best side," Maya explained, stopping and posing like she was in front of a group of snapping paparazzi.

"Maya, what size is that dress, and can I borrow it please?"

"Nina, did you hear something?" Maya pulled her shades slightly down, looked around the room, and then pulled them back up, covering her hazel eyes.

"Do either of you not understand that I gave you that key for emergencies only?" I stated, looking from Nicole to Maya.

They both burst out laughing and gave each other a high-five. "Nina, keep it real. The only emergency you've ever had was when you tried babysitting your sister's cat, and it ran out in the street because you left the door open," Maya said amused, giggling to herself. It was a secret that I'd made Maya swear on her life to never spill.

"Nina! You said Chaka was kidnapped," Nicole pouted, snapping out of her shock. Maya shoved her back down, waving off her tantrum.

"Maya, you promised to take that secret to your grave. Sorry sis, but Chaka was a handful, always tearing up my clothes and scratching me. You'd leave and she'd turn into the spawn of Satan."

"That's the last time I ask you for a favor. Wait, did you lose Mr. Charlie too? Momma said he was sick and needed to be put down. Now I'm rethinking her excuse." Nicole bounced her knees up and down.

"Nicole, sweetie, you change clothes, occupations, and ideas like you change your underwear. You're the last person who needs to question responsibility. So, can we discuss *me,* please?" Maya clapped her hands together in excitement.

"What has you so excited, besides the latest sale at Barney's?" I snickered walking to the kitchen to grab a bottle of water before practice.

"Well, since you've asked. I have my first exclusive interview with the Gage *'Billionaire Catcher'* Young!" Maya squealed in her seat, clapping with glee.

"Oh, can I come, please? I won't interrupt you at all," Nicole pleaded, getting down on her knees and holding her hands clasped together as if in prayer.

"Good luck with that, hopefully he won't be a jerk during the interview," I spat.

"From what Shelly said, he's a sweet guy. You have any food? I'm starving after doing rehearsals all day." Maya stood and hightailed it to the kitchen.

I pulled her back by the end of her coat and made her sit back down. "No, go home and cook for yourself. You and Nicole eat me out of house and home." *Damn, I sound like my parents,* I thought, shaking my head wearily.

"Ignore her, she hasn't had sex since Dorian and her broke up. You know lack of sex is turning her into an old grumpy woman. The type that just sits in the house watching all the neighbors go in and out of their house, being nosy and telling everyone's business," Nicole taunted using her hands to simulate having sex.

Flipping her off. "Nicole, unlike you, I don't have one-night stands when a man buys me a Happy Meal and a toy. I'm a grown woman that looks for a guy with substance, goals, who knows what he wants out of life. Someone who can keep a job for more than a year."

"All right, I need you two to focus on me, and what I

need in this moment. Have you talked to your cousin, Jimmy, about me?" Maya inquired once again. She'd always had a crush on him since we were little. At least once a month she'd ask me about him, or ask if we have a family function coming up where she'd jokingly flirt with him excessively. Unfortunately, Maya was too spoiled, shallow, and obnoxious. Jimmy liked his women a little more humble and less feisty. Don't get me wrong; she was my closest friend, but she'd break my cousin's heart if they got together and dated.

"Jimmy is not your type. You're more Gucci, and he's more Old Navy. My cousin is too good for you, honey. Sorry, boo," Nicole said, gathering her purse and opening the door as we followed her.

Maya glared at me with a side-eye, pouting like a petulant child. "Nicole, as the youngest one in the group, can you raise your hand in confidence and say that you've never had an STD? Oooh... that's right, you can't. So, don't speak on who's better than who, baby girl," Maya challenged as we reached her candy-apple-red, two-door Porsche Cayenne.

Nicole followed me over to my Honda Civic and slid into the passenger side in a huff with her arms crossed.

"Ladies, the last thing you two should be doing is getting into an argument. Leave Jimmy out of this and Maya, we're heading over to my parents for dinner. Are you coming or what?"

"No, I have a date. Tell your parents I said hello, and tell Jimmy the next time you see him, I'm ready for that date," Maya taunted my sister, driving off while sticking her tongue out and honking her horn.

* * *

"Hey, Dad, Nina yelled at me earlier today about my lack of morals. Where's Mommy? I feel a headache coming on. Once it hits, you know my chakras will become misaligned." Nicole stormed right past me and into the house.

Our father chuckled to himself, leaning down to hug me. His six foot two height still intimidated most people. Along with Nicholas Jr. and Grandpa Donald, all the men in our family were tall. As for me, I stood at five feet and six inches. In heels, I could easily hit five nine.

"Nina, how are you, baby? I haven't seen you since Sunday dinner a month ago." Grandmother Doretha gestured for us to sit down. Her favorite pastime was playing cards, especially poker. She was shuffling a deck with *Wheel of Fortune* playing quietly on the big screen TV. Most of the family knew not to play against her based on her habit of cheating. She also wouldn't let you live it down if you lost during a game against her enemies, which mainly consisted of her church members. She loved showing us off to them too, talking their ears off about her granddaughter being a former college softball player, her grandson, a former football player in the NFL.

"Grandma, sorry I haven't been around much. Work at the center, plus coaching the softball team has been taking up a lot of my time."

She leaned over and pinched my cheeks. Picking up two cards, I watched as she maneuvered the hands before Grandpa came into the room.

"Hello, my sweet NiNi. What the hell has happened to your sister? She's in the TV room laying across the couch holding her hand across her forehead. Chanting 'I am Peace, I am Peace,'" Grandpa Donald said, imitating Nicole, and bent over laughing holding his stomach.

The door opened and Nicholas walked in with Romi following behind him holding a stack of folders. I stood up, hugging Nicholas, and grabbed a few of the folders out of her hands and rubbed her baby bump.

"Look at you, Romi. Your little bump is so cute. How far along are you now?"

"I just hit the four-month mark. Your brother is so overprotective I can barely do anything without him being near me," Romi said, in a hushed whisper, pulling me back toward my old bedroom.

"I told you when you got with Nicholas that he's the alpha-male type, mixed with a little beta. He's the supportive, calm, and quiet type, but once you mess with his family—especially his woman—watch out because the beast will come out," I replied and Romi nodded her head in agreement, sitting down on my bed.

Romi sighed a few times, rubbing her belly and staring up at my old softball jersey. I smiled. Those were the good old days. I played for the New York Eagles National League. Trophies and plaques from that time still sat proudly displayed around my room.

She placed a hand on her forehead, rubbing her temples.

"What's really going on with you, Romi? I can sense some friction with you both," I asked.

"It's the community center. Some big time company is trying to buy the land and turn it into a shopping mall or something, and your brother's stressed with trying to figure out a way to keep the center afloat. You know how he likes to handle problems on his own. I feel like he's not communicating his frustrations and keeping me in the dark and working long hours," Romi stated, rubbing her temples.

There was a gentle knock and my mother walked in.

"Here you two are—hiding out in the back, leaving your grandmother to get on my nerves. Come on out here, dinner is ready, and you need to feed my grandbaby," Mom said, shaking her head and walking off leaving the door wide open.

"And everyone questions where Nicole got her issues from. I say look at the mother," I said, linking arms with Romi and heading to dinner.

Once dinner was finished, I drove over to the community center to print out the lineup of kids with parent information before practice tomorrow.

The lights were still on and I saw Ramone, the security guard standing at the door. He's an older gentleman that's worked at the center since it opened. Reminds me of my dad with his bowlegged walk, tall height, and sprinkling of grey hair, not only on his head, but his beard as well.

"What are you doing here so late?" Ramone questioned holding the door open and moving aside to let me inside. I passed him a plate from our dinner tonight.

"I wanted to get supplies counted before practice on Monday. How's the family?"

He locked the door and followed me down the hall toward my office. Unlocking the door, I entered the office to grab the lineup sheet. Walking out of my office, I took the key off the board handle and went down to the dugout.

"You need me to go with you?" Ramone asked.

I waved him off and walked further to the dugout. Picking up the chart, I opened the cage that held the sports equipment. Turning the side light on I counted and moved the base mats together. Two minutes later, my phone vibrated and I pulled it out of my jacket and noticed I was tagged in a Twitter post. Clicking the link, it showed a photo of a woman and that jackass on the ground from a celebrity gossip site with a headline called "Is she the girlfriend?" Always wrong place and wrong time. Which reminded me, *I still need to be reimbursed for my phone.* I mumbled to myself. Deciding to not engage I blocked the website from my page and closed out of the app. Finishing up tallying the equipment, I locked my office to head home; my plan was to open a bottle of wine and maybe catch up on *Good Girls*.

Chapter Four

Gage

My agent called me this morning talking about the latest photos on Celebrity Trend's gossip site. He was going on about me getting caught up with all these women and not staying focused on my game. Tailynn and two of her friends, Celine and Kaylee, were sitting in the back watching her favorite BTS music video on her tablet. Samantha and I switched off every other day on dropping her off and picking the girls up, along with the other moms; it was this whole Mommy and me carpool thing that she'd signed up for that I had no clue about.

"Breaking news! We have a potential new outfielder in negotiations to join the New York Raptors. We'll bring you more details as they become available."

I turned the radio off so that I wouldn't have to hear the sports announcer's usual gossip as I pulled up to the school in the carpool lane. My car windows were tinted, and my license plate said GYCATCH. The entire school knew that it was me who drove Tailynn like this. I loved just being her dad and not a famous athlete, but the few times I showed up to her school, it became a big issue, with fans and photographers waiting outside for us. She'd been embarrassed about me ever since and I hated it.

Even after her mom and I broke up, Li'l Bit understood that we loved each other and would always be a family, but our lives would be spent in two homes now. Plus, the bonus Christmas gifts didn't hurt. Then, Jason came along two years ago, capturing her heart, and he and I also got along really well. Somehow, Li'l Bit had turned into a well-adjusted kid, one who loved the color purple, her friends, family, and softball.

Eventually, she wanted to play in the major leagues, like me, and my heart couldn't fly higher. I promised that I would do everything in my power to attend her practices and games as much as possible, and give advice if she wanted to make this her career. My focus was on making sure she got enough playing time to grow as an athlete and decide on her own what she wanted to become when the time came.

At the end of the day, as her parent, I didn't want to push my dreams on her the same way my family tried to force me into taking on the CEO role in the family business. The financial world was not my cup of tea.

And speak of the devil as if they heard me talking about them, here they were blowing my phone up.

Father: *We need to meet.*

Daniel: *Don't try to escape, Gage. It's important that we show a united front, as a solid company. You need to show your face around here a bit more.*

I groaned. I hated it when they hounded me with bullshit that they knew I didn't want to be involved in—especially if it had anything to do with the business.

Me: *I'm on my way*, I replied heading into the line at the crosswalk of the school. Tailynn opened the door and all the girls piled out, grabbing their backpacks, and waved goodbye.

Heading in the direction of Young Industries, I turned the radio up and listened to some old-school hip-hop to keep my mind clear so I wouldn't spaz out on my family. Tobias Young was your stereotypical, spoiled rich man who lived simply to make money. He was born into wealth and instilled in my older brother, as well as my younger brother Gordon, and me, the value of staying rich by any means necessary. I didn't want to live like that though.

Pulling into the building, I didn't feel like parking in my reserved spot, so I passed the keys over to the valet instead. I wasn't planning on staying long. I still needed to get my tattoo freshened up and head over to Tailynn's practice after she was done with school. This meeting better not take all day. Depending on my father, it was the same speech of having a responsibility to the family business and making sure we keep the Young family name relevant and on the map.

Not wanting to wait in the security pat-down line with the other visitors, I walked through and headed onto the elevator, and then up to the twentieth floor.

The bell rang and I stepped off as dazzling smiles stayed glued to everyone who looked my way. That's the other reason I stayed away from coming up here. All of the women flirted, even though they knew I was the boss's son.

I opened the door to his office without knocking. My brother sat in a chair in front of my father's desk.

"Why was I summoned?" I demanded, wanting to

dismiss with the pleasantries and get right down to business.

Daniel, the oldest, who was married with two kids, sighed at my annoyance. "Sit down," Daniel ordered, pointing at the second empty chair in the room.

"I'm good," I responded.

We'd always had a contentious relationship growing up. He was disappointed because I stood up to my father's bullying to some degree and stuck to my passion, rather than being forced to become involved in the family business. He was envious to some degree, and thought I was the golden child of the family, and he was always seeking approval from our father. I stuck with being independent and not living dependent on their name and money. Sports had always been my first love and I worked hard enough at it to get a scholarship and then become a star athlete. He didn't see what I saw; growing up our father was pitting us both against one another for his own greed and manipulation. Gordon, the youngest brother, was being groomed, and hopefully, he'd learn early on that this lifestyle brought nothing but headaches.

"Gage, take a seat, son," my father said. Tobias Young didn't look a day over fifty, even though he was in his early sixties. He just closed on another property in New Jersey and was constantly scoping out some other property. His business was known for buying up property for cheap and flipping it for a higher price or demolishing it and building high-rise condos.

Closing my eyes and counting to five, I tried to let go of the anger that rose up in me whenever I was in this place with them. I opened them back up and walked over to sit down in front of his desk.

"We found a property that we think would be perfect

for the expansion of our next group of luxury condos. I want you and your brother to go and visit with the owners to see how much they are willing to let it go for and report back to me," Father arrogantly stated, passing a cigar to my brother, and offering one to me.

I shook my head, and he shrugged nonchalantly.

"Call up one of your goons to go meet with them," I told him. "I'm busy, and if you haven't heard, I don't work for you," I said.

"You don't, but this business has afforded you and my niece many luxuries. Besides, the local businesses would rather have a visit from you more than they would some guy in a suit who has no ties to the community," Daniel explained.

Shaking my head, I jumped up and paced in front of his desk. "The corporate world has nothing to do with me. Whatever company you're trying to steal from keep me out of it, because I refuse to help," I informed him, waving them off and striding to the door to leave.

***

Pushing through the doors of Talbot's tattoo shop, I noticed a few of my team members and Jason huddled in a corner, laughing, and talking to Talbot. The entire block was somewhat of a hangout, since Jason's shop was next door, along with a few of my favorite restaurants.

I felt my phone vibrate. Taking it out, I noticed a text from Samantha, reminding me to drop Li'l Bit off at practice today after school.

Samantha: *Don't forget about her practice, and be nice to Coach Mitchell.*

Me: *How many times are you going to hound me about this?*

Samantha: *Until I hear from Tailynn tonight about her day.*

Me: *I'm up here with your fiancé. How about I tell him about your ice cream problem?*

Samantha: *You wouldn't dare.*

Me: *Keep bugging me about her practice, and Jason will find out all about your dirty little secrets.*

Samantha: *I really don't like you sometimes.*

Me: *I love you, too. Now, leave me alone.*

Samantha responded with a GIF of one of those reality housewives rolling their eyes. I turned my phone off and shook hands with Jason, Caleb, and Marcus.

"Don't get all cocky with Tailynn's coach today. Also, remember to get her cleats before you pick her up from school; she left them at her mom's place," Jason said.

"Am I on one of those hidden camera shows or some-thing?" I fussed, looking over my shoulder, checking the light fixtures, and all the pictures on the wall.

"G, what are you doing?" Marcus asked.

"Trying to figure how the hell everyone keeps coming at me about being nice to some coach that I could not care less about. First it was Samantha, now Jason. Anybody else want to throw their two cents in about me?"

"Well..." Caleb started to explain, but I cut him off with a hard glare.

Everyone started laughing, and I shook my head in annoyance.

"How many times did I tell you about bringing your friends with you to my shop?" Talbot stood with a cigarette in his mouth, pointing over at the crowd of paparazzi who were standing in front of his shop, blocking foot traffic.

Pissed from earlier today, my temper was at an all-time high, and I knew it would only get worse as the day continued.

"Man, ignore them. I need my tattoo freshened up."

"What has your panties in a bunch?" Talbot asked, turning to walk back to his station as I followed behind.

Diya was sitting at the receptionist desk and I waved hi as she was talking to Scottie. I assumed she must have just had something done because she signed off on her pay stub.

"Take a seat. And which one are we recoloring?" Talbot wondered, grabbing a fresh pair of gloves.

I sat down in his chair, pointing to my arm with Tailynn's name that was fading. "Family," I answered, blowing a breath out in aggravation.

He moved his chair over and grabbed a fresh needle, checking out my arm to see what needed to be done.

"Rough day then?"

"Man, you don't know the half of it. I still need to head over to Li'l Bit's practice. How long have the boys been here?"

"About an hour or two."

Turning me so the light was shining in the correct direction, Talbot sterilized the area and started to work on the tattoo.

"How is she doing?"

"Man, she's my whole world. Samantha signed her up for softball and I have to pick her up from school and take her to practice after this. She loves playing. I wish I had known earlier on when she first started because I'm just now getting involved with her playing."

"Never too late, and knowing Tai like I do, she'll love the game. So, what happened with your family? I know things are good with Samantha, right?" He inserted more ink into the needle, tracing the outline of Tailynn's name in cursive on my arm.

"Tobias found another property and wants me to go and try greasing the wheels to impress the owners."

"How many times have you done that for him?" Talbot muttered, wiping the excess ink and blood off my arm.

"This will be the tenth time, if I agree," I recalled, feeling the sting of the needle.

"Are you planning on doing it this time? You should talk with Genesis; maybe he can talk with your father about finding different arrangements."

"You're right. Genesis is good with the business side of things; he knows that world way better than me. The man went to Davenport Business School."

I contemplated his idea. I knew how persistent Tobias could be, and he *did* have a little clout with the owners of different teams, so I knew that if I denied his request, I would need to really handle the backlash and not get caught up in his web of lies.

"We'll see, but I forgot to tell you about this woman I met. Talbot, she's fucking beautiful, a little feisty at times, but I can handle it and she knows baseball like the back of her hand, she's not just one of those women that fakes it simply to impress me."

The constant hum of the needle halted, and he stared up at me.

"Please don't tell me you went out with Elizabeth, the two-time divorcee that's shopping for another husband like she hits up Saks?"

"Hell no! I bumped into her while I was on my date with Elizabeth actually. If I ever get married, which is not even a priority for me right now, if it was to Elizabeth, it's because she drugged me or something. Besides, she's too loud during sex."

"I thought you only had one date with her?"

I usually don't kiss and tell with my boys about the women I sleep with, but I knew I could trust Talbot not to go around and spread my business. I ran a hand down my face, thinking of how much to divulge. "We kind of hooked up after our failed dinner date."

Talbot burst out in laughter. I scowled at his reaction. "She got her claws into you now, my friend," he noted, shaking his head before turning the tattoo gun back on and continuing with the line work.

"It was only the one time, and I blocked her since then because she was talking crazy, about wanting to meet her parents and all these long-term plans. I was like, "Sorry to these parents," I joked, impersonating the social media joke the actress KeKe Palmer made go viral. Talbot and I slapped hands chuckling at my comment.

"So, this chick you bumped into, what's she like?"

"Shit, we bumped into each other twice, once on my date with Elizabeth and then again at the gym. She must be well known or something because the gym is exclusive for celebrities and VIP clients. Damn, I just realized I didn't get her name. Anyway, she's around five foot seven I think, and petite, with a kind of an athletic built, but still curvy and shapely. Her hair was in a normal messy bun, kind of like the ones that Samantha does for Tailynn. She has a cute button nose and plump pouty lips that when she looks angry or pissed off it made you want to bite her bottom lip, and when she challenged me, damn."

"Dude, are you getting turned on right now?" Talbot scolded with a grin on his face.

"What, no!" I waved him off, and he laughed and continued with the tattoo.

Talbot turned the needle off and scooted back. "Do you need to go rub one out or something? Because I'm not tattooing you until you've calmed down."

I growled, annoyed that he caught me and I felt like a sixteen-year-old again and getting caught by my parents with a girl in my bedroom.

Chapter Five

Nina

Monday rolled around and Nicholas stood in his office with his back to me, staring out the window at the cleaning crew as they were busy setting up the field for softball practice. Romi had recently redecorated Nicholas's office at his old high school in his professional league colors as a birthday gift. A few of his trophies stood on a mantel next to a photo of him and Romi. A family reunion photo with all of us kids and our parents hung proudly on the wall. A jersey with his retired number was framed and hanging on the wall, next to a photo of me in my playing days.

"How are you feeling about things?" I asked, moving in closer to stand next to him.

"I'm good, sis. Thinking about what our next move should be and hopefully these lawyers can get some answers soon."

He stuck his hands in his pockets. I leaned my head down on his shoulder, and he did the same. We were always close growing up and this was our family's dream of opening more community centers around the city and the surrounding area one day. If we couldn't bring in more funds before these corporations put an injunction in, then I worried about the validity of the plan. Despite popular belief, women in sports really didn't make that much money, especially in the softball field. I had a few endorsements, but all of my money went mostly into helping keep this place running from payroll, bills, and supplies.

"How's the baby?"

"Good. Romi's driving me crazy with her cravings, but so far, we're good. Healthy and she's even thinking of starting her own business."

"Really?"

He nodded in answer. "I told her I support her, but the timing isn't right. We have this place to deal with and then the baby, plus, I want to propose and have a wedding after the baby is born. The stress would be too much for us."

"I hear you, but you know Romi can handle it, and Nicole's not doing much these days so maybe she could help."

"Maybe. What's up with Maya and her dramatic ass these days?" he asked, moving away from the window and sitting down at his desk.

I perched on the edge of the desk remembering that Maya wanted to do a dinner with the girls sometime this week. I had to try and fit that in and all our schedules were crazy at the moment. I groaned in anticipation of what he was about to say. I knew my brother hated being in setup situations with trying to hook his friends up. I knew Maya had a little crush on his friend, but I didn't expect her to do anything irrational. But then again, what am I saying? This is Maya we're talking about.

"Working on building her ratings. Lately she's had the opportunity to go to a few red carpet premieres to interview celebrities. I know she wants to do a girls' night out and possibly a trip here pretty soon."

"Yeah, she needs to stick to causing less problems with some of my friends in the entertainment field. That gossip show will only cause her to get more hate than love. They think because you're my sister and she's your best friend I can make her stop. I need her to slow down on the name dropping, because it's causing my boys to not have happy homes."

"No one can control Maya. All I can say is I'll talk with her, but I make no promises. Oh, by the way, guess who I ran into and almost cursed out?"

"Who?" he questioned, his breathing quickening, ready to jump up and fight my battles.

I patted his shoulder in an attempt to calm him down. "I can handle him, I promise. It was that famous baseball player, Gage Young, or whatever his name is. Bumped into him when I went for a grocery run a few days ago, and he was on a date, I assume. Then again when I was at the gym, he tried to spit game."

"Oh Lord."

"What!"

"The last time you dated an athlete it ended up with me and Pops barely keeping you from busting his head in with your bat. Please do us all a favor and don't go down that road again," he said, shaking his head. My mouth hung agape at his response, flushed in embarrassment at the remembrance of Jeffrey cheating on me with my college roommate. I caught them in the act literally as she was on top of him grinding away and I was coming in from class, and I heard him scream out my name. I stepped out of the dorm room to double-check the door number to make sure I wasn't going crazy and he moaned my name again. I can laugh about the whole situation now, but back then I was pissed to the fifth degree. We fought for a while prior to that, because he felt my time was spent on the game and less on him, so he decided to go out and find comfort somewhere else. I'd called Maya to let her know to get bail money ready, and I figured that once I hung up, she called my dad and brother because they both burst through the door not even ten minutes later, trying to talk me down from killing them both.

Sliding off the edge of the desk I waved off his chuckling at me.

"Alright, so I freely admit I have a bad track record with dating athletes. Gage is the last person I would ever date anyway. He's too arrogant and spoiled. Both opposites that would never work."

"You know what they say right?"

"What do they say?" I replied with air quotes.

"Opposites do attract," he answered and I flexed my middle finger up and watched as his mouth hung open in shock. I walked out of his office striding outside to get ready for practice.

I'd scheduled the practice for the little league girls softball league. This was my second year of coaching since retiring from the game.

"Kelly, can you make sure Jaime has her cleats this time? Her mom forgot to pack them last week. Also, don't let anyone on the field—especially the parents. They tend to try and run the show. Last year, I almost got into a fight with someone's mom because she thought her daughter needed more playing time—completely disregarding the fact that she was failing two of her classes." I pointed around the field, directing my assistant coach, Kelly, over to the small equipment stand.

I swear, parents always wanted a superstar athlete for a child—never mind them having an education, I thought. A few feet away, I could see some parents gathering in the bleachers, talking, and mingling while the kids piled onto the field. It was a nice, sunny afternoon on a Monday in New York, the best time to get in some practice as the school year was winding down. Most of the practices happened twice a week, typically on Mondays and Wednesdays. Then, Saturday mornings, we had official games. All of the teams in the league were named after their respective foundation, so our team name was Kids Kare.

"Hi, Coach Nina!" I heard Tailynn scream as she ran toward me, wearing her softball uniform.

Bending down slightly, I gave her a hug, then pulled away and tapped the top of her helmet with her name written in gold glitter. "Last time I checked, you didn't have this glitter on top of your helmet, young lady."

"I know, I asked my daddy if he could get mine designed like his so we could match."

"Oh, pretty nice. I may have to have your daddy do mine as well."

Tailynn nodded.

"Tell Daddy what you need, and he'll make it happen, babydoll." I froze at the voice and the hard body pressed up right behind me, disbelieving that he was there. I tried pretending that I was on that old TV show, *Bewitched*, and I blinked once, twice, and then three times, but still nothing changed.

"Is something wrong, Coach Nina? Your eyes are acting funny," Tailynn inquired, putting her hand on top of my shoulder. I smiled and stood back up turning around, and staring at the asshole himself.

"She's your daughter?" I demanded, crossing my arms. He stepped in closer, effectively taking up any personal space that I intended on having.

"Babydoll, I came to play. I see we keep meeting like this, so it must mean that fate is saying that we should get to know each other," he answered, grinning mischievously, rubbing his hands together.

"Don't call me that, and this is a kids' game, Mr. Young...?"

"Gage...Gage Young and you must be the infamous Coach Nina Mitchell that Li'l Bit talks about all the time," Mr. Young responded, stretching his hand out for a shake.

"Mr. Young, do you not believe in personal space?" I queried, taking a step back and not shaking his hand until he discreetly pointed to Tailynn staring between the two of us. I uncrossed my arms, smiled, and shook his hand in return.

Tailynn smiled and ran off to the dugout to get ready for practice.

"You can go now, Mr. Young."

"Gage."

"What?"

"My name is Gage, not Mr. Young, or better yet, you can call me Daddy." He winked showing off a sexy smirk, knowing it would piss me off. This guy being Tailynn's father was going to be a problem. A problem I didn't need at the moment.

"I'll call you Mr. Young, same as I do the other parents with kids on the team."

"I'm not like the other parents," he whispered, leaning toward my ear, and closing the space between us again.

Clearing my throat, I took a step back, putting space between us.

This was the third time we'd been in the same space, and I needed to make sure I established a professional relationship. Gage was extremely handsome, but I knew that those types of guys only wanted one thing, and I wasn't about to be on another person's list. "Go sit in the bleachers with the other parents, please."

"What's your team ranking for the season?" he questioned, crossing his arms over his chest.

"If you must know, we're currently three and eight."

He mumbled under his breath, "losers."

"Excuse me? What did you just say?"

"Listen, I play this game professionally. You should put my girl in at shortstop."

"And you should stay out of the way, like the other parents. I'm the coach of this team," I stated, glowering.

He groaned. His features contorted into an anguished grimace. "And yet, you're at the bottom of the league," he responded with a hint of sarcasm.

"Mr. Young-"

He smirked. "Gage."

I folded my arms. "I'm not calling you Gage."

"Want to bet?"

"You don't have anything I want."

"From the looks you were giving me the other night, there's a lot that you need."

"Coach, the girls are ready to line up," my assistant called over, effectively interrupting our back and forth bickering.

"Okay, get them started on some running drills."

Feeling a headache coming on, I rubbed my temples. I wanted to smack that cocky smirk off his face. "What does that mean exactly?"

"It means your little toy. How about this, you put Tailynn in and if she excels or improves during practice for the next two games, let her play in that position for two games and then I'll sit quietly in silence for the rest of the season."

"And what do I win if she doesn't make a hit?"

"Instead of using the toy, I get a kiss?"

"Why would I let you kiss me on the lips and how is that a win for me?" I sassed in response, arching an eyebrow and crossing my arms over my chest.

"Who said anything about your lips up top? Obviously, the ones below need a little more attention, based on your toy preferences."

My mouth hung open in shock. Before I could respond, Tailynn ran over.

"Daddy, make sure you get a good seat to watch me," Tailynn said, effectively breaking our tense standoff.

Soon, more parents filed into the bleachers, clapping and screaming. Gage walked over to sit near my assistant and staff in the dugout, pointing to the field trying to give plays, letting his proposal hang in the air like a cloud.

Not wanting to show any interest, I shifted away from my disbelief and continued on with practice.

"Okay, girls. Amy, you go to third base; Bridget, you're the shortstop; and Tailynn, I want you to catch," I explained, blowing my whistle, clapping my hands, and directing the girls into position. I heard a loud whistle. Looking over my shoulder, I saw Tailynn's father shaking his head, as he sat in the dugout.

Amy was at bat and Patrice was up to pitch. I blew

the whistle and the girls started up today's practice. Looking back over my shoulder, I saw that he had left the dugout and was talking to one of the other parents, and she of course was giggling at everything he was saying. "Out!" I heard the umpire scream and I turned just in time to see him jump up for joy at winning the first round of the bet. I wasn't planning on kissing him, let alone going out with him. I focused back on the girls to do another drill. This was silly, and hopefully he didn't put the cart before the horse because this was going to be a two out of three games in order to keep this bet going. He walked toward me and stuck out his hand.

"What's that for?" I questioned, watching the grin curve into a beautiful set of pearly white teeth.

"It's just good sportsmanship to shake hands to start the competition. Like I said, if Tailynn continues to improve and wins during practice, then I get my kiss and you have to go out on a date with me."

"Slow your roll on the date part and you've got yourself a deal." I gripped his hand and we shook on our agreement. He pulled me into his chest.

"You smell good, babydoll."

"Don't get used to my smell."

"I'd love to answer that in a sexual way. But, I'll start off keeping it PG for now."

✳✳✳

Stopping by to see Scottie at work, I noticed Diya and Genesis.

"I see the party is here at the office today," I challenged, canvassing the wall of pictures where all the magic happened at Scottie's Hour, an online blog and radio show.

"NiNi, isn't this a pleasant surprise," Diya said.

Genesis hugged me and I waved to Diya and sat next to her in the chair.

"Nina, I have to tell you Celine is loving softball. You ever think of going back to play again?" Genesis remarked, rubbing up and down Scottie's arm.

"I tell her all the time. You remember how we met?" Scottie challenged.

Diya, Scottie, and I giggled at the same time remembering our first encounter.

"I have to hear this," Genesis insisted.

"As you know, Genesis, your wife tends to do outlandish things," I commented.

He nodded in agreement and Scottie threw her head back in laughter.

"Diya and I met first from at the mall, because I was thinking of getting a tattoo, rebelling against the status quo. Then one day, I bumped into Scottie and she knew my mutual friend Emery Stone the wife of Pierce Motors owner Jackson Pierce. As I debated getting my ex-boyfriend's name tattooed, this one here overheard me complain about him at the same time."

"I can only imagine what she said," Genesis echoed in a loud, long, exaggerated sigh.

"She said if you get his name tattooed on your body and he's not living up to the standards you've set for yourself, then sweetie you're a fool." I mimicked Scottie's stance the day of our first encounter.

Diya fell out in a belly laugh.

"That's my girl," Genesis replied.

"Was I right?" Scottie asked, smiling coyly.

"I see why she handles all the responses for her radio question and answers," I explained.

"That day she ended up not getting a tattoo and we all went out for drinks discussing the men in our lives, and the rest is history," Scottie said.

"I have to get going, I wasn't planning on stopping over. Just wanted to say hello," I informed, standing back up to head out for the day.

"Don't forget about the dress for the auction," Scottie reminded me.

"I won't. Let me get out of here and get some rest. Bye ladies, and Genesis, try and keep her out of trouble."

"We are talking about Scottie Maguire, right?" Genesis gestured to his wife.

Diya and I glanced at Scottie, shaking our heads in jest as she waved us all off.

* * *

One hour later I arrived home. Turning the ignition off, I rubbed my temples stepping out of my car and headed inside. Entering my condo completely exhausted from the day, I stood against the door for a moment closing my eyes. It galled me to have to admit that he was right. Bridget was the worst shortstop I had ever seen. I didn't have the heart to tell her mom how bad she was. And at the same time, I didn't want to give in to his stupid bet either.

Tonight, I was looking forward to catching up on reality TV, drinking wine, and eating popcorn. After talking to my brother about the money we needed to raise, we figured that participating in the fundraiser would help. Genesis family threw a charity event every year to help raise money and this year was a bachelor and bachelorette auction. Scottie, Diya, and Nicole talked me into going up on stage to raise money for the community center. Taking the key out of the ignition and grabbing my bags and paperwork, I walked inside my condo and nodded at the security guard, Joseph. He was an older gentleman who had been retired but started working again since his wife had died.

"Hi, Joseph, how's it going tonight?" I asked, picking up my mail.

"I'm good, Nina, how was practice?"

"Great, the girls are getting better every day," I replied proudly, heading toward the elevator. A few minutes later, I walked into my condo and decided to call my girls to catch up on the latest gossip. Forty minutes later, I was showered and on the phone with Maya venting over today's events.

"So, how are things at practice?" Maya inquired. She was on FaceTime with me as I watched the latest episode of my favorite show, *Girlfriends.*

"Fine. Besides Gage literally trying to run things and us constantly bumping into each other, he just so happens to be the father of one of the girls that I coach. Maya, he made a wager and wanted his reward to be a kiss, and I quote *not the top lips, because the bottom could use some assistance,*" I repeated snarkily, then listened as she cackled on the other end of the line.

"Oh my God! He must know your ass has been dry down there and that vibrator collection can't replace what a real life man can do for you."

"Shut up! I can't stand you. I'm so embarrassed, Maya. I'm this close to banning his ass from future games."

I heard a loud thump echo in the background and I screamed her name to see what happened, but all I heard was raucous clapping and peals of laughter. "Nina! Child, you are too much. How are you going to ban one of the richest men in baseball from attending his child's game? In what world does that make sense, boo?" Maya replied.

"In mine, and stop laughing at me. This is serious and I need your help. Oh, and Nicholas wants you to slow down on posting about his friends on your show."

"Nicholas, and his friends, can suck my-"

"Maya!"

"It's my show, and he needs to worry about Romi and the baby and less about me. Unless he's realizing what he's missing?"

"Focus on the task at hand. I'm not saying to not be yourself, just be careful with what you're posting. Some of these people take things too far. Anyway, I need advice about my situation."

"I hear you and I'll try harder with keeping certain things under wraps. For your situation it's easy, I say get laid and be happy."

"This is why I'm determined to find new friends. Between Nicole and her get rich quick scheme jobs, and you trying to live the life of Wendy Williams, I need to have more stable friends and family."

"Now what fun would your life be without us?"

"No comment!" I joked and hung up on her, ignoring her calls as she tried calling me back. I turned my phone on silent and headed to bed.

Chapter Six

Nina

I had Celine on the mound and Gloria was up at bat. Mr. Young was standing off to the side this time watching with his arms crossed over his broad chest. He talked me into another stupid bet again and I didn't even remember how it happened. Celine was one of my best players. Diya, another girlfriend of mine, introduced me to Tailynn's mother, Samantha. We found out we're all friends with Celine's parents, and we've all been friends ever since.

"Gloria, chin up and legs steady on the plate. You got this!" I encouraged, as I spotted Gage leaning down as he talked to Tailynn standing next to him in her outfit ready to go out onto the field. Celine tossed the ball and Gloria fouled out once, twice, and then finally struck out. Her head down, looking crushed, along with myself. I groaned with my head in my hands, knowing he was going to make this torturous.

"So, it's looking like the count is two to one in my favor huh?" Gage stated lustily, licking his lips, standing right behind me.

"I wouldn't get too happy, Mr. Young."

"I'm telling you, take it from me and I can have you guys whipped into shape in no time, but that is only if you take my advice."

"I need a drink."

He chuckled as Celine and Tailynn ran up toward us. Gage stood next to me with a smirk on his face.

"Daddy, you see Celine strike out? I'm going to get a hit and run next, just watch and see," she happily stated. He nodded in agreement, rubbing her shoulders.

"I know, Li'l Bit. Keep doing what I told you about keeping your arms at an even space and watching the pitcher to be in sync."

Tailynn hugged her father, and went running back off onto the field as Celine went to go grab a bottle of water.

"Let's take a five-minute break!" I yelled and waved for everyone to come in and grab water.

"Do you plan on not fulfilling your end of the bet?" he commented, walking beside me as I went to the dugout to check the next lineup of kids. I looked up, hearing my name called and spotted Romi heading over to me. Ignoring him, I hugged her and let him sulk behind me.

"Hello, who are you?"

"Nobody."

"Gage Young." We both answered at the same time. Her eyebrow lifted in confusion.

"Okay... Nobody Gage Young. Wait... I know that name. Aren't you the famous baseball catcher?"

"I am, and you are?" he answered, stretching out his hand to shake hers.

Nicole had called me about five times back-to-back, and text messaged about an emergency. So, I decided to cut this little introduction short and make sure my sister was all right. Whatever gloating he wanted to fling at me could wait.

"What's up, Romi, you need something?" I insisted walking away from prying eyes. His piercing eyes stayed locked on mine and I blushed at his determination to be in my presence. *No, you are not falling for the whole okie dokie ma'am thing,* I thought to myself.

"He's cute, Nina."

"Nope. Stay focused and don't fall into the trap like Maya and everyone else that calls themselves my bestie, and trying to hook me up with a cute face and hot body," I say, snapping my finger in her face to turn back around and focus on me and him.

"Ohh. He must be really getting under your skin, boo. You're all sweaty and your pupils are dilated. Girl, don't run from your blessings," Romi said waving shyly at Gage as he walked up to the pitcher's mound with Celine. I assumed that he was giving her tips and tricks by the way all the girls circled around him.

"Gage is the last person I would ever go on a date with. Now what do you want so I can keep him from rigging my game?"

"Nina, it's a kids' softball game...anyway, Nicholas told me to tell you to look at the list of banks he wants to try and meet with. All of them are stating it'll take weeks to get an appointment in person, let alone to process a loan application."

My phone buzzed again and I checked seeing another message drop in from Nicole. "I have to check in with Nicole, she keeps blowing my phone up. Tell Nicholas to send me the details and I'll make sure to look them over." I hugged her and rubbed her growing baby bump. I sighed as I turned. Making my way back over to the field, I scrolled through my contacts and dialed my sister's number.

"Hello?" Nicole answered.

"Hello, are you all right? What's the emergency?" I asked. I held up a hand to Gage to let him know that I needed a minute.

"Are you still at work?" Nicole questioned.

"Yeah. Why?"

"Come to the house, I have a surprise for you."

"What! I thought something was an emergency."

"When you get here, you'll see," Nicole said cryptically and hung up the phone before I could reply.

"Are you ready to admit defeat?" Gage teased, standing up, practically towering over me. The chemistry between us was intoxicating and I needed some air. Even though I was outside, just the sight of his bare arms in the white t-shirt, and the Nike jogging pants showing off his imprint, which I suspected was nice in size based on all the tabloid gossip and women that spoke out about his prowess in the bedroom, was enough to make me feel like I was walking through a sauna with how flushed my body felt.

"I will never admit defeat. We have a best out of three, so this time instead of the girls, what do you say about me against you at the batting cages?" I announced setting myself up to win part two and finish removing that smirk off his face. Everyone knew I was the best at the batting cage. He was probably like all the other men in thinking a little softball player couldn't match up to the big league players. Throughout my career, people have always underestimated me until I showed them who I really was.

* * *

It was going on seven p.m. and normally we finished around eight-thirty with us looking over plays together as a group. Nicole had my mom calling me, like the house was on fire or something unless I showed up immediately; so I ran over and left my assistant in charge of practice. As soon as I got in the house, Granny explained the real reason they'd gotten me over here. As usual, Nicole thought she could help fix my life while completely ignoring hers.

"Nina, you didn't hear it from me, but Maya, Nicole, and what's her name—Diya—are upstairs. Supposedly, you have a blind date. Again, you never saw me, baby, but they set you up on a blind date," Grandmother whispered conspiratorially, looking around the room.

"Sis, you look tired," Nicholas told me, walking into the room with Romi following close behind. They had left the center before me talking about having dinner plans. Come to find out it was all a setup.

"What is your crazy sister up to?" I demanded.

"Nicole is on some love thing at the moment and trying to hook everybody up instead of focusing on her own life and getting a job," Nicholas said.

"While I've got you here, Romi told me about the whole thing with the bank, do you need me to bring anything in particular for the meeting?" Nicholas was thinking of putting up his house as collateral to potentially get a second look at our case. The center was an older structure; it'd been in our family for years and was started by our grandparents the year they got married, and we received the greater majority of our operating revenue from donors and the community investments. Disappointment washed over his face, and he grasped Romi's hand. He gave me a look and leaned in to kiss Granny on the cheek before starting to leave. "Pops thinks we should take it to court. Tomorrow we'll talk more, but for now, just go have fun and enjoy yourself," Nicholas said, letting Romi walk through the door first.

"Okay, Nick, I'll come find you when I make it into the office tomorrow. Granny, where are they?"

Nicole yelled from upstairs and she didn't even need to explain what my night would be like.

***

This was not the emergency I was thinking she needed my help for, and having me leave my practice to come here on a bogus setup for a blind date was too much. I rolled my eyes at all of them. I can admit it's been a while since I've gone on a date, making me feel like I was completely inept with finding a guy to go out on a date with me. That was not the problem. Men only wanted one thing, and I'm not in the mood to deal with a guy that only wants sex on his terms. The restaurant we were supposed to meet at was my favorite, so of course she knew I wouldn't just up and leave. "Nina, sit up straight; this dress is about showing off your boobies," Nicole teased, cupping both breasts and pushing them up. The wonder bra she had me wear helped keep them high and perky—even though I knew that once the bra came off, it was a totally different story.

Diya, Nicole, and Maya called Scottie to meet us at the restaurant, and they sat around with me waiting for my date to show up. Nicole had found him on the "Bachelor's Life" app for single women. They made a fake profile and thought he'd be a perfect match for me.

"That red dress looks sexy on you, Nina. It reminds me of the time when I tried to make Genesis jealous and went out with Emery's best friend that happened to be a singer," Scottie said.

"Do you mean that time you had Emery's best friend, Daiton, singing at dinner to get Genesis jealous to break up with you?"

"No one's asking you to marry him. It can't hurt to get some dick out of the guy though," Scottie insisted with a wink.

"Preach!" Maya fist bumped with Scottie, as Nicole chuckled at them both.

"Believe it or not, there is more to life than sex, ladies."

All four women gasped, and burst into laughter at my comment.

"Oh, here he comes, ladies," Nicole said, pointing over my shoulder.

Even before he walked up close, I smelled the strong musk of his cologne. It was a mixture of wet, moldy laundry, garlic, and a three-day-old pizza.

The look in Diya, Maya, and Scottie's eyes told me all I needed to know. The guy stood in front of our table. I ran my eyes from the bottom of his shoes up his diminutive five-foot five frame. He smiled with one gold tooth, a fake toupee on his head, and a thin mustache that needed to be trimmed and held the remnants of whatever he ate for lunch in the patchy strands.

"Tony, right?" Nicole asked, holding out her hand for him to shake.

"Damn, it must be my lucky night to have so many

beautiful ladies waiting on me," Tony flirted, kissing Nicole's hand, and she giggled.

"Tony, this is my sister, Nina, the one I was telling you about."

"Fraud!" Maya joked in a coughing manner at Tony's blatant flirting.

Diya and Scottie stood up without shaking his hand and grabbed their purses.

"Where are you two going?"

"The babysitter called; I need to get back home," Scottie lied, attempting to hold back her laughter.

"I rode with her, so I need to get back to the tattoo shop. You have a nice date, NiNi."

"This was your idea; you can't leave me now," I demanded as Maya stood along with Nicole.

"I have a date of my own, so don't stay out too late, Nina—and don't do anything I wouldn't do," Maya taunted, moving around Tony, and pointing at his toupee. Nicole pushed her, gently herding her toward the entrance and Maya held her stomach, chuckling all the way out of the restaurant.

Chapter Seven

Gage

"Mr. Young, I hear you're single but still very friendly with your ex. Is that true?" Maya asked during the interview on her show, *Spotlight with Maya*. She was beautiful in a Tyra Banks type of way. But her attitude was extremely self-centered. I couldn't date someone who only thought about herself and the designer clothes she wore.

"If you mean co-parenting and close friends, then yes we are."

"You started dating in college, correct?"

"We did, but I don't make it a habit to talk about my private life, Miss Armstrong."

"Call me Maya, Mr. Young, we're all friends here."

I chuckled at her 'all friends' comment. Maya thought I was new to gossip and media shows. But I'd done my homework on her, and I knew she was after some juicy gossip about me still sleeping with Samantha—which I wasn't, and I hadn't been in a relationship with her for years now. I kept Tailynn and Samantha out of the media for a reason.

"I don't doubt your three million viewers are all friends of mine."

"That is true. Based on your reputation, you are written about a lot because of your attitude both on the field and off, from dating multiple women to calling out your fellow players and being the son of a very high-profile and unlikeable man, who's trying to buy up a lot of property in certain neighborhoods."

"Was there a question in there?" I asked, as my eyebrows furrowed. She grinned, shifted in her seat, then tapped her pen on the index card holding all the questions.

"Mr. Young, what do you have to say about your family removing local jobs from low income businesses?"

"No comment."

"What about the insinuations from your fellow team members about you being overrated as a catcher, since the team hasn't won a championship in two years, and you're currently ranked third in the National League East?"

"No comment."

"Um, Mr. Young, the way this works is I ask the questions, and you answer."

"Then, ask me something worth answering."

She narrowed her eyes in a grimace. I wasn't supposed to put her in the hotseat, and that was probably pissing her off. "Your daughter, Tailynn, is currently playing on a softball team, correct?" she asked, adjusting her seat.

Grinning, I decided to let her off the hook for a second and answer one question. "She does, and I'm super proud of her. I just need her coach to see her potential and put her in the starting lineup."

"Are you saying she deserves to be in the starting

lineup simply because she's your daughter, or because she can actually play well?" Maya goaded, trying to get me caught up in a gotcha moment that would play on social media around the clock, unless I moved the conversation in a different direction.

"My daughter should play starting position because she works hard and she's good at the game. I've always instilled in her a strong work ethic and that things won't be handed to her simply because she's my daughter. The coach is stubborn and doesn't understand when she has a star in front of her, and to nurture the talent she has been entrusted with."

"I can see that you care a lot about your daughter, and about being a father. So, naturally you should want what's best for your child. So, please clear up for our viewers why your family is in the process of displacing local businesses that will lay off hundreds of workers—some with children as young as your daughter—just to make money that we know your family doesn't need," Maya spat, leaning forward and entwining her hands.

"I'm not involved in my family's business."

"But you do benefit from it, correct?"

"How long have you been a host of your talk show, Miss Armstrong?"

"What does that have to do with my question?"

"Answer the question."

She rolled her eyes, clearly not wanting to be put on the spot. "To answer your question, I went to school, and after a year, I dropped out to focus on entertainment journalism. A friend had an opening in the online department, and I worked my way up to host her show, and then we rebranded it as my own show," she answered.

"So, you're basically saying that a friend helped you

get into this position, like a family member would do?" I suggested, and she started to connect the dots as her eyes hinted at understanding where I was heading with this.

"You're good, Mr. Young; I'll give you that. But it doesn't help the audience understand why things aren't looking good for their jobs."

"It's unfortunate that's what is happening, as you implied. But I can assure you that I'm not involved in my family's dealings. Not the way you think."

Her gaze bore into mine. The room went silent before someone motioned to go to commercial break.

"We'll be right back with more from Gage 'Billionaire Catcher' Young on *Spotlight with Maya*."

The camera shifted down, and a makeup artist walked up to Maya, dabbing her face. An assistant gave her a bottle of water with a straw inside, which I assumed was so that she wouldn't mess up her lipstick.

"You're not slick, Mr. Young."

"I have no clue what you're talking about."

She blew a breath of arrogance out then waved for her assistant to step away.

"This show you're putting on, trying to make everything seem like it's not as bad as it really is. Your family is trying to shove local mom-and-pop shops out of business. For example, many local business owners have written into the show about the practices of some of these large corporations and how they bulldoze out smaller business with offering to buy the property at low costs, offering no relocation fees and then even going so far as to raising costs of living with new high-rise condos that we don't need. How much money will it take to satisfy your family's unquenchable thirst for money?" she admonished, standing, and leaning down into my face, pointing a finger at me and chastising me like a child.

"Listen, I'm sorry about your friend, but that has nothing to do with me. Now, if you want to finish this interview, then I advise you not to make it personal, Maya," I said as she glared at me.

A countdown clock started, and the intro started back up as we both stared at each other, neither of us willing to break.

"Mr. Young, I want to thank you again for being here with us today, and I have just one other question for you before we let you go. I have a lot of single women that watch our show and I know they're wondering if you're single?" Maya smiled, a total pro in letting the earlier intense conversation roll off her shoulders.

"I'm single and dating right now. Nothing serious—even though the gossip blogs like your show tend to have me married with ten kids on the way every other week," I responded with a practiced smile.

"All you single ladies, you heard it here on *Spotlight with Maya*—Mr. Young is single and very available for a date, if you're looking. Stay tuned for my after-show on YouTube, where we discuss all hot topics," Maya stated, holding her hand out for me to shake as we called a truce for the camera.

"Cut!" a producer yelled, and the bell rang, signifying that the on-air sign was off.

* * *

Her voice sounded firm and steady. She teased me by slowly and sensually kissing my dick. "Was this part of the bet, Nina?" I moaned out, gripping her hair tightly as she slapped my hand away.

"Baby, you lost, but that only meant I wouldn't be able to pleasure you, and you know how much I like feeling your cock inside me after getting him awake." Nina giggled, popping my dick out of her mouth. The water dripped down her plump ass and I bent over to squeeze and smack it, as she pumped and twirled her lips around my cock. We were standing in the shower after a day at the park running around with Tailynn and her friends. Nina and I had a bet that if she won, I would wake her up with oral sex every morning for a week. To me that wasn't a bad thing, and if I won, she would give me head for a week.

"Fuck!"

"Say my name," Nina whispered.

"Baby! Your ass is mine."

"We'll see about that," Nina moaned, as I came all down her throat.

"Shit!" I shouted, waking up out of a dream. Sweat drizzled down my face and chest.

I sat up in bed checking the time on the nightstand. "I need to win this bet," I muttered out loud as I tossed the covers off of me, and headed to the bathroom to cool my raging hard on with a cold shower.

Chapter Eight

Gage and Nina

Gage

I parked in the underground parking garage of the batting cages of Baseball Extreme studios. A place that had t-ball, mini-golf, and other kid friendly events. Plus, there was a restaurant inside. Nina was already here and meeting me inside, her assistant coach gave me her number after I promised to give her seats to my next game. Normally I wouldn't pursue a woman, they always came after me. Somehow, Nina got under my skin and I couldn't let go, or at least get her to realize that I wasn't just some playboy that dated and slept with women and didn't want to be committed. Well now that I'm older, I've come to know that the wife and the white picket fence was something I could honestly see for my future.

Stepping inside I noticed Nina in the waiting area talking on her phone. I walked over to her and pulled her into a hug.

"He's here now, Nicole. Yeah, I'll call you later. Okay." She spoke quickly hanging up the phone.

"Who was that?" I questioned walking her over to the counter to pay and get our section.

"My sister," she responded, having no idea how sensuous her voice sounded.

"How many siblings do you have?"

She tried to pay for herself and I glared at her and the cashier. She shrugged and put her money back inside her purse.

"Two, what about you?"

"Two, I'm the middle child," I said placing my hand on the small of her back, escorting her to the area we had reserved outside in the back corner away from prying eyes.

"Me too. I have an older brother, Nicholas, and a younger sister, Nicole. Often times, I feel like the one that my parents are constantly relying on to handle everything that happens in our family."

We walked over to our reserved section and she passed a bat and helmet over to me.

"Same. I always felt like the responsible voice of reason in the family especially when something important happened and neither of my brothers wanted to deal with it."

Nina

"So what where you like in high school?" I asked him, letting him step up to the plate first.

"Ladies first," he insisted.

"Nope, you first, Mr. Young."

He smirked and put money in the machine to get it ready for the system to start.

"If you must know, I was a normal kid growing up,

into sports, hanging with my friends and dating. Nothing out of the ordinary." The first ball launched and he hit it on first contact.

"I can't imagine you being a one woman type of guy."

He missed the second ball and turned to look at me.

"If you give me a chance, you'll find out a lot of things about me. I'm not that bad, Nina. Even if the media makes it look like I'm some rebel playboy." He passed the bat toward me to set up and I gripped the helmet.

"How about friends for now, and we will see where things can go." The pitching machine started up and I hit each ball that came out of the system. I turned and grinned as his mouth was wide open in shock.

Gage

Three days after the interview, the press was having a field day with our family. Photographers questioned me at practice, hung out at my condo, and followed my family around. My brother called me on the same day the interview aired because his kids were getting hounded at school.

"Why the hell would you do an interview that paints us in such a negative light?" he'd asked me.

Eventually, I had to turn my phone off. I tried to stay out of the corporate side of things. I never wanted to be grouped in with that world of corruption. I might have been an asshole, but I did have a heart and seeing families lose their jobs wasn't an easy thing to stomach.

It was a breezy afternoon, and I was fresh out of practice, driving over to meet with my father and brother at the office. My father had summoned me to make an appearance today because it was apparently my fault that people knew about what he was doing. Afterwards, I had to meet up with Li'l Bit at her practice. Samantha had texted me earlier to ask if I could pick her up because she had a fitting for her wedding dress that she couldn't skip.

Turning into the parking structure of Young Financial Industries, I parked in the reserved space for me that was next to my father and brother's. Even though I didn't have anything to do with the business on a day-to-day basis, I still had to come in and sign paperwork every once in a while, or vote on certain things, so I had a permanent space.

Stepping out of my car, I shut the doors and waved to the security guard. I entered the building, passing through security.

Tailynn was at practice at the community center across town. I had learned since the interview that Li'l Bit's coach was Maya's friend, Nina, and The Mitchell Community Center was a well-known name in the community. If my father was good at his job—which I knew he was—then it was currently about to be uprooted. And there wasn't a damn thing I could do to stop it.

Chapter Nine

Nina

I was excited to get a new pack of batteries to use my new toy. After that disastrous date, and everything that was going on at the center, I needed a lot of time to work off the stress. I had my red wine on the table, Marvin Gaye playing low, and was freshly showered. This was my third vibrator in the last six months. Lowering my panties, I turned the vibrator on low, easing it down to my lower lips. I started to tease when suddenly, there was a knock at the door.

"Go away," I yelled, trying to concentrate.

As I continued concentrating, a moan left my lips. Another knock came from my door. I placed the vibrator under the pillow, and jumped up to answer the door with frustration.

"Oh my God, what are you doing here? Do you understand boundaries?" A frown of puzzlement briefly marred my face.

"Your mail was left in my box by accident, and if I recall, you lost a bet," he pressed, standing arrogantly in the doorway with his arms crossed over his chest and my mail in his hands sticking up. I didn't want to admit that he looked sexy, like he just came off a runway. I can't believe he lived in the same building as me. Snatching the mail out of his hands, I glowered at him and turned away placing the mail on the table.

"Mr. Young, I don't know what type of girl you're used to, but I'm not one of them." I attempted to shut the door, but his foot stopped the door from closing.

"Do you play hard to get with all the guys? I spoke with your friend, Maya, and she told me a few things about you. Like, you're defensive and stubborn ever since you broke up with your last boyfriend—I believe his name was Dorian?"

I turned and walked to the corner table near the loveseat, and he walked in behind me and shut the door. "It's a nice place here."

"Are you stalking me?"

"I'm your neighbor in the penthouse remember? I saw you walking in with a few bags the other day, and I paid security to find out your apartment number," he explained, taking a seat on the couch.

Exasperated from his blatant intrusion to my privacy, I sat beside him, glaring.

"So, about that bet—Li'l Bit is excited about being the new shortstop. She wanted me to invite you to dinner at our place."

"As nice of a gesture as that is, I can't do it. I don't mix business and pleasure."

"I'm liking this outfit better than the one you were wearing when I first saw you. You're sexy when you're angry. He must've really done a hell of a job to get you to hate *me*."

"I don't hate you. I just don't like you. Sorry I'm not one of the girls that will just fall all over your words."

That statement was about to start an argument, probably. I'd tried turning my vibrator on low, but it was still going off. We both looked around, perplexed at the noise. Attempting to hide what it really was, I insisted he get out of my apartment.

"What's that noise?" he asked, glancing around the room.

"I think it's my oven." I jumped up, trying to pull him along toward the door.

He shifted out of my grasp to investigate the noise. I watched him, horrified, while he looked around the room disturbed by the loud buzzing sound. It must have been on the highest level you could turn it up to, a setting called, *honey, let it out*. He was looking behind the couch now, under the table, picking up the pillows, and I started coughing, hoping to distract him, when all of a sudden, he noticed the vibrator.

Fuck, I thought to myself.

"So, you're just hanging out with yourself, not hating me, while you use a vibrator in the shape of a dick," he taunted, holding it in front of my face.

I reached out to grab it, and he pulled it back out of my reach, up above my head while I jumped for it.

Finally, I stopped, pissed. "All right! Yes, it's mine, okay? I like the vibrator; I use the vibrator; and I embrace the vibrator. Every woman should have one because you can't depend on a man. Now, if you will excuse me, I need to get back to masturbating—and as far as your bet goes, we're even. I will see her at the next game."

"And what about dinner at my place? Don't forget, I did win the first bet."

"I'm not having dinner with you again."

"So, then I want a kiss," he demanded nonchalantly, stepping closer to me.

"Fine. One kiss, with our eyes open, hands kept to our sides, and no tongue," I answered, moving in close and attempting to figure out how I could make this the worst kiss possible and not regret it for the rest of my life. I had a rule of not getting involved with athletes—let alone someone who was a parent of one of my kids on the team. The media storm that could come from this situation was not something I needed.

His gaze lingered over me. I took a deep breath. I hid the vibrator behind my back and pushed him out the door, shutting and firmly locking it behind him.

* * *

"I think you should have sex with him, Nina, you haven't had a little fun, letting your hair down with a man in a few years and this way you'll get your little drought over with and have an on call sex appointment with a man of your dreams," Nicole spoke, taking a bite of her grilled cheese sandwich.

We sat outside at Borders Grill—a little mom-and-pop restaurant. I had the afternoon off and she wasn't doing anything at our parents' house but ordering more clothes with money she really didn't have.

"I see you've been talking to Nicholas lately."

She shrugged her shoulder, not caring. "You're my big sister and I want you happy. I know after you left from playing the game and went to work for the community center you didn't really have any time to meet anyone and focus on your love life because of work. The center will always need something, you have to put yourself first sometimes."

"And you think standing up there on stage letting men bid on me is the way to get lucky?" I inquired, taking a sip of the honeydew lemonade. I ordered a grilled cheese sandwich with a side of fries, and she ordered onion rings, which we ended up sharing. I admired her metabolism because she devoured whatever she wanted and never gained any weight. Me on the other hand, I fluctuated if I never worked out, even during the season while we played. I was petite, but still thick around the hips and thigh area.

"It will be fun, Scottie, Diya, and Maya have talked about what you should wear and maybe you'll catch the eye of someone special."

"Or maybe I'll just stay home and get a second job to help the family."

"Boo! You're no fun. Please, I promise if you do this, I won't bug you about borrowing some of your clothes."

I laughed. "Nicole, you still haven't returned my black leather jacket from last year, and you expect me to believe you'd stick to your word on this? I was born at night, just not last night, baby sis."

"Okay, what if I promise to be your assistant for a week, no two weeks? Plus, cook you dinner."

"Make it a month and I'll think about participating."

She huffed and frowned in annoyance. After a few seconds she grinned and stuck her hand out to shake on the deal.

"Deal!"

"Why do I feel like I'm setting myself up for trouble?"

Chapter Ten

Nina

His thumb stroked across the aching point of my nipple. I arched in silent invitation.

Gage teased my lips with his teeth, nibbling them ever so gently before he nudged them apart so that he could explore every inch of my mound.

I gasped.

"This sweet pussy belongs in my face every minute, every hour, of every day, baby."

I reached out to grip his hair as his beard tickled across my inner thigh.

This was so wrong and felt so right. I told myself I wouldn't go down that road again with dating an athlete. All they caused was heartache and drama with baby mamas, traveling, and long distance. Now look at me bent over my couch with his head between my thighs.

"Shit...faster. Ughhh!"

Slap!

His large hands came across my ass as my juices flowed down my inner thigh.

Ring!

Checking the clock on the nightstand, I saw that it was two a.m. After tossing and turning, I couldn't sleep. I'd had a wet dream about Gage after his searing kiss—which I could admit had me tongue-tied. His soft lips and strong arms had me floating on air. I pushed the covers back and sat up in bed. The damn vibrator had only made it worse because now I wanted the real thing. I turned on Netflix to try and distract myself from all thoughts of Gage. Getting involved with a man that high profile would only cause a distraction. Having the media attention and gossip bloggers hunting my trash and disrupting my life because they assumed I was dating some famous athlete was not a road I was willing to travel.

I wasn't planning on participating in the charity auction theme this year of a bachelor and bachelorette auction that Jackson and Genesis co-sponsored every year, but Nicholas and Nicole had convinced me to put myself up on the block. In their minds, it would help with bringing funds to the community center, but I didn't consider myself famous; women in sports received one-third of the fame and fortune that their male counterparts earned. Gensis family are big donors with helping raise money for homeless shelters, and community center when we needed a school bus for transporting for away games, and they made it a point to support women in sports, and especially kids. It was just one of the reasons they fell in love, and became even more so from how he took on the responsibility of Celine once he found out she was his daughter. I appreciated them, but at the same time, I didn't want to take advantage of our friendship.

Pushing the covers back, I decided that I needed air to get my head space right. I picked up my phone and checked the latest news. Dragging my feet, I headed to the kitchen to grab something to eat and drink.

I saw a text from Nicole about not forgetting to get a wax and manicure before the event. Emery was in the group chat with her, Diya, and Maya since the other wives were busy.

Emery: *Don't be nervous babe.*

Maya: *Work on your oral skills.*

Me: *Maya, get off my phone.*

Maya: *What did I do?*

Diya: *Dead.*

Nicole: *She's not saying anything we wouldn't all say.*

Emery: *She kind of has a point. Have you seen the guys that attend these events?*

Diya: *She's nervous enough, let's not scare her.*

Me: *I...*

Maya: *I knew it! You slept with somebody?*

Nicole: *You worked on your oral skills?*

Me: *Can we move on from oral sex please?!*

Nicole: *:(*

Diya: *You set yourself up for that one.*

Maya: *If it's not about sex then I'm leaving the chat.*

Me: *It's too early, and I need some sleep.*

Nicole: *See you in the morning.*

Chapter Eleven

Nina

Nicole and I were driving over to the venue for the auction tonight. I knew in the back of my mind that it was nuts to try and pull something like this off with the rest of the girls and their spouses tonight. We had an injunction submitted for the time being, and hopefully a miracle will be pulled off. The money we raised tonight, I hoped, would be enough to buy the entire building, but whatever happened I wouldn't give up on saving my family's business.

We were greeted by flashing lights and reporters asking questions, and I noticed Emery and Jackson smiling together as he held her close, along with a few other people I knew. The annual fundraiser was being held at the W Hotel tonight. Most of Genesis's charity events ended up selling out, and seeing so many of my friends made my heart swell. Seats by themselves typically cost around fifteen hundred dollars per person. Maya was meeting us there to help me get changed into something for the bidding. I was nervous about whom I would win a date with, but as long as it wasn't Gage

Young, I guessed it would be all right. The publicist had sent out a photo of some of the guests who would be in attendance, and I hoped like hell that I was last on the list to go up. Earlier, I'd spoken with my parents and brother. He said he'd be waiting for my call to see if we received any funding. Granny had even left a message on my phone, talking about bringing her some grandbabies home, but that was the last thing on my mind.

"Nina, you remember my husband, Jackson?" Emery introduced us and I shook his hand.

"How could I forget, nice to meet you again, Jackson. Thank you again for supporting my family's center. I know you usually have these things set up months in advance."

"Emery has spoken very highly of you, Nina. The work you're doing with the girls' softball team is amazing, and I'm thinking of signing our son up for next year if you have a team for boys or co-ed," Byron admitted, releasing her hand and kissing Emery's cheek. The opportunity to meet people in the racing sports world, that I admired and helped to get her husband on board.

"Nina, we need to go inside and find our seats, and you have to get changed," Nicole mentioned, reminding me of what we needed to accomplish tonight.

"Emery and Scottie! Over here! Who's your friend?" a photographer demanded loudly.

"Do you mind posing with us, Nina? This would be good publicity for the center," Scottie explained.

Glancing around at the crowd, their publicist motioned for me to stand to the right of them, with Nicole on my left. We all smiled and posed for the cameras as the shouting continued. Suddenly, I heard yelling and a commotion erupted. Turning to the right, I saw Gage getting out of his limo and buttoning his suit jacket. He didn't notice me, so it was the perfect opportunity to hide.

"He looks like a whole snack," Nicole blurted out, and the publicist next to us agreed with a nod of her head.

"Remember, Nina, this isn't about you; it's about the kids. So, the more cleavage you show, the better," Nicole hinted with a wink, adjusting my breasts in the low-cut cocktail dress that stopped at my knees.

Maya had sent me to the best hairstylist in the business—a friend of a friend who was married to her very own rich man. My hair was in a high ponytail, and I wore large diamond earrings that I'd borrowed from Maya. We wore the same size-six shoe, so she'd let me borrow her light pink heels.

"He can't be serious!" I shouted, dropping the curtain to close off anyone from seeing us. This was supposed to be a small fundraiser; no one had told me that it would be broadcast around the world.

"What's wrong?" Maya wondered, looking out into the crowd, and smirking at what I knew would be the worst mistake ever if Gage won his bid.

The makeup artist checked the last-minute touches on my lipstick. The crowd was large; lights and cameras were in the back. So many famous people and athletes were milling about in the crowd.

"I'm not doing this," I stated, crossing my arms over my chest, and striding back to the dressing room.

Maya stepped in front of me, blocking me from going back to my dressing room.

"Remember why you're here, NiNi," Diya said, checking her vibrating phone.

"I am, and this won't work. Maybe we can put in for a small loan or –" Maya cut me off before I could continue.

"Nina, you're hung up on that man. Why are you talking yourself out of going out on a date? It's not like you have a lot of eligible guys starting a bidding war for just the pleasure of your company," Nicole rattled off, tossing her hair behind her back. Today, she was dressed a little more conservatively, with a long, straight, blonde wig, a long, red-and-white dress with a slit on the side, and a shawl covering her small chest.

"You have to bid on me," I blurted out, figuring out a plan to get out of going on a date with any of the players.

"What?!" Maya shouted, glancing first at Nicole, then at Diya. They all looked at me strangely, like I was crazy.

"Between you and Nicole, I won't lose if you two make sure no one bids on me. Besides the price won't go up over five thousand based on all of the previous bids tonight."

"Nina, your plans usually don't turn out right. I think you should just suck it up and go on the date with whoever wins," Diya responded, grinning because she knew that I didn't want to end up on a date with Gage.

"Her problem is that she's scared she'll be sucking, based on the person that wins," Nicole mumbled. Maya giggled, slapping hands with her at my expense.

"Okay, enough laughing. Go out there and get ready to bid. No matter what happens make sure you win."

"I'm broke, so I can't bid on you. This dress cost me two thousand dollars, and I agreed to give my date a little special treat tonight for a ticket," Nicole answered, walking off to sit at her table.

"Ladies and gentlemen, we are here today to raise money for a variety of charities. I want to make sure everyone goes home with significant funding. So, there will be a bachelor and bachelorette auction starting in just a few minutes. All our eligible bachelors and bachelorettes will have one date with you to the location of your choice. Some rules will apply, but more than anything, let's have fun and get those checkbooks out," the auctioneer announced.

"We need to take our seats. Have fun and smile for the men," Diya said, following behind Nicole, who sat at a table with Gage.

"Maya, you have to help me. The last thing I need is a date with Gage. We have nothing in common, and he's an ass."

"The old saying goes, if you're this upset at a man that's not your man, then you must like him," Maya said, patting me on the shoulder.

"The next bachelorette is a retired athlete from New York. She's currently the coach of a softball team and works at the Mitchell Community Center..."

Chapter Twelve

Gage

The Young family kept a table at all the major charity auctions in New York. Pierce Mortors had partnered up with the league to do a dating auction.

Nina crinkled her nose at me. I couldn't wait to put a bid in on a date.

I sat at the table with Jackson, Genesis, and Emery, whom I'd met a few days ago. She was just as feisty as Nina. A few of the players from the team had come, along with Jacob and Samantha.

"The starting bid is five thousand dollars for a date with Nina Mitchell, do I hear five thousand?"

Raising the paddle high, I made sure to get the first bid in as she stood there, looking completely annoyed with me. Her friend, Maya, raised her paddle. The announcer pointed at her response.

"We have one for five-thousand, can we get six-thousand?"

I smirked at her confidence. She thought I would give up. I lifted my hand to match the six-thousand-dollar bid.

"Mr. Young matched the six-thousand dollars, do I hear seventy-five hundred?"

Maya held her hand up to outbid, and then another man yelled out, "ten-thousand dollars!" Everyone in the room was shocked by the outburst.

The waitress came around with a tray of champagne, and Scottie leaned over to whisper in my ear, "She looks beautiful; good catch, Gage." She grabbed Genesis's hand, giggling at my expense.

"Twenty-thousand is at the highest bid going once." An older ball headed guy winked holding his paddle.

"Fifty-thousand!" came a voice from across the room.

"Oh shit!" Maya yelled.

No man was going to outbid me and win a date with Nina.

"One-hundred thousand!" I stood up and shouted toward the stage.

The entire room went silent, except for the furtive whispers taking place all across the room.

"Maya, do something," Nina whined, motioning for her to bid again.

"Sorry, Boo, I don't need a date that bad, have fun with your man," Maya testified.

Nina tried to cut in on the announcer.

"Two-hundred thousand!" Robby, another player on my team shouted, standing up, grinning, rubbing his hands together.

"Genesis, who is that jerk trying to outbid Gage?" Scottie asked, pointing at the guy who was always trying to take what I had. Unfortunately, he could never be me.

"Sweetheart, everyone here is bidding; we can't call him a jerk if he just so happens to outbid our friend," Genesis calmly stated.

"Of course, *you* would stay all calm. Diya, we need to help Nina," Emery insisted, digging into her purse, and pulling out her phone.

"Nope, not happening." Jackson said, taking the phone out of her hands and her jaw dropped in surprise.

"Five-hundred thousand."

The entire room gasped in shock.

The microphone dropped.

"Get it, Gage! Claim your girl," a girl that showed a resemblance to Nina screeched out.

Nina's stare intensified.

"We have a bid of five-hundred thousand going once, twice... sold! All details will be finalized at the door," the announcer explained.

Nina walked off to the back and I followed behind, leaving everyone gossiping as the flashing lights went off.

Having my price showcased all over wasn't ideal, but I needed to be alone with her, so we could establish some type of friendship.

* * *

The door almost closed behind her, but I stuck my foot out to prevent it from closing, then walked in and closed it behind me, locking it to keep any distractions from interrupting us. "Wait, Nina. Let me talk to you for a minute."

She held her hands up to stop the words. "No." Nina snatched her clothes up and kicked off her heels.

"Answer me this, Nina, are you afraid to be alone with me or afraid you'll actually fall for me? The trip would be fun, we could have dinner on the beach, do some fishing, sightseeing, and shopping? I'm going to make sure this date gives us plenty of time to get to know each other. What better way to do that than having our date be a long weekend out of town, or whatever."

"How often do you get a headache?"

"Not often why?"

"Because from the arrogance of your comments, I can tell that the size of your ego must really cause a burden on your brain. The last thing I would ever do is fall for you. This little bidding war does nothing to change my mind about going out with you," she snapped, heading to the bathroom.

"Don't forget your bathing suit!" I yelled, leaving her alone to change.

* * *

Loud jeers and clapping in the smoky bar pulled me out of my daze as I drifted back to earlier. I texted the guys to meet up after the auction, mainly just so I could vent.

I just wanted her to take me seriously. There was just something about her. And she played ball? And this whole thing with my father and brother trying to take over her community center. No wonder she hated me. I needed to gain some perspective. I needed some advice with how to make my little plan work once I got Nina alone.

Everyone was still wearing tuxes from earlier in the evening. Marcus had a date with a fashion designer who had bid a lot of money on him. The gleam in his eyes once he locked in on the person who'd bid on him showed he was definitely intrigued by her.

"Was it worth it?" Marcus probed, taking a sip of his tumbler of whiskey.

"What? The auction?"

"Yep. That girl Nina seems a little tough to crack, and you aren't the best when it comes to having relationships. Nina would probably run you ragged with her attitude."

"Are you talking about Scottie's friend?" Genesis coaxed, taking a handful of peanuts out of the basket.

"Please tell me they don't know each other?" I asked, annoyed. If Scottie was friends with Nina, then I knew the sassy, stubborn, take-charge attitude would be something that could be a problem in the long run.

"When Emery and I first got together. That woman was tough—and still is—and she's fiercely protective of her friends. I hope you're serious about Nina and not just looking for a one-night stand because my wife would not take to you hurting her friend," Jackson warned, passing me another beer.

"I got another problem that I need some help figuring out."

"Does it have anything to do with your father?" Talbot concluded, looking over at the screen with a shot of Marcus hitting a homerun.

I blew out a harsh breath of frustration, nodding at his statement. I ran a hand down my face.

"He wants me to help put them out of business, and Daniel is up there pushing this whole 'you need to support the family business' bullshit right along with him."

"So, the auction money was helping keep them in business?" Marcus remarked, slipping a fifty-dollar bill to the waitress as a tip. She winked, and he passed his phone number over.

"It should, but I don't put anything past my father or brother. Hopefully getting her alone with me so she can see the real me will help. I'm not trying to throw my money around. More just showing her that there's more to me than my baseball status, I'm planning on taking her around the beaches, sightseeing of the caves, exploring the food and people."

All the guys shook their heads.

"What?" I shouted as they burst out in laughter.

"Gage, you're the most arrogant son of a bitch I've ever met, and that's coming from me. Pride and ego combined is a hell of a drug. Don't block out your blessings," Genesis said, standing up and putting another hundred dollars on the table.

The days of us being playboys were coming to an end. My goal was to leave this island having made Nina my woman.

Chapter Thirteen

Nina

Tailynn, Samantha, and I sat with chocolate face masks on in the spa room. They'd invited me along to hang out and I felt honored to get to know his daughter off the field. The trip to Fiji was coming up soon. Gage told me he planned for us to swim in the ocean, go sightseeing, eat, and talk more about ourselves and less about media perceptions. I didn't know how Samantha felt about things. So, once we finished here, lunch was on the agenda. I hoped I could talk to her and get a read on things.

"Are you having fun, Tailynn?" Samantha took the cucumber slices off her eyes and peeked over at Tailynn sitting in the chair as she got her toes done.

"I am, Mommy. Are we going shopping after this? I told Celine I was getting the new Ivy Park shoes."

We both choked on our cucumber water at the same time. I loved B like the next fan, but some of the pricing on celebrity clothing was insane and ran around a hundred bucks or more for just the smallest item.

"With what money, Tailynn?" Samantha replied.

"Duh, Daddy's of course."

"He has her so spoiled it's crazy." Samantha said, hiding a grin and rolling her eyes.

"Same as my little sister. She has no filter, and our parents spoil her with whatever she wants."

"Speaking of your family, how are things going with the center?"

I sighed at her question. I really was trying to avoid anything that had to do with the center today. "A work in progress honestly. We can talk about it later, I'd hate to spoil our time together, by talking about business."

"You know, Gage is excited to take you on the trip," Samantha chuckled at my unamused response about Gage and the trip.

"It was the only way he could get a date with me I guess," I shrugged my shoulder nonchalantly.

"He told me about your little best of three agreement or something. You're good for him, and you keep him on his toes, I think you should give him a chance. I know it may sound weird coming from me."

"It really is." We both broke out in laughter.

"Gage is a good guy underneath that macho exterior. How about we all have dinner one day, you and Gage, with me and Jacob, or is it too soon?"

"Let me think about that. Who knows? I might hate his guts after this trip and never want to see him again," I whispered lowly so Tailynn wouldn't hear.

Samantha winked, and we continued on with our day.

* * *

The next night, Gage showed up to my place with bags of takeout.

"What are you doing here? Is that Chinese?"

I let him walk inside as I closed the door. I'd just gotten out of the shower and only had on my night shorts and tank top, with a scarf around my head holding up my curls after coming from the salon.

"I finished practice and had ordered more than enough food to share, and since Tailynn was with her mom, I decided to come and hang with you."

He followed behind me to the kitchen and I opened the cabinet grabbing plates and utensils. He removed the food out of the bag and started to place the orange chicken and veggies on our plates.

"You have enough food for an entire baseball team. What's really up? Did your date cancel on you? I see three boxes of orange chicken, pork and veggies, fortune cookies and noodles."

"No date, just a friendly dinner between two people. I know the fundraiser was a shock, but I like you, and Tailynn likes you."

Opening the fridge, I pulled two bottles of water out and we walked into the living room to sit down on the couch and eat.

"How does that make you feel? The fact that the people I care about like you?"

"Surprised, shocked, annoyed, nervous."

"What are you nervous about?"

"You."

"I don't plan on hurting you, Nina. This trip is meant to be fun, and if anything happens, it's by your choice," Gage answered in response.

"Did Tailynn tell you I went on a spa day, and shopping with her and Samantha?" I asked, effectively changing the subject.

"Did you guys have fun?" Gage questioned, grinning.

"I did," I answered in a nod, stealing a piece of orange chicken off his plate.

He looked around the room and under all the pillows before answering.

"What are you doing?"

"Checking for your vibrator to make sure you pack it for the trip."

I tossed the pillow toward his head and he caught it before it landed on his plate and we laughed in unison.

Chapter Fourteen

Gage

One week later...

I knew that keeping my father's secret with being behind the acquisition of her family's community center would cause problems. Seeing her face when I won the bid at the fundraiser reminded me that she only thought of me as some arrogant, cocky, playboy bachelor. Honestly, it was true that before her, my life was about Li'l Bit, baseball, and getting laid without any commitment.

Fiji Island was always beautiful and I made sure to have all the essentials that she needed from hair products, the favorite soaps she liked, and clothes for everything I had planned. I'd paid for seclusion away from the resort traffic on the other side of the island.

"What do you think?" I was trying to get her to let her guard down now that we made it here.

She wasn't quiet on the plane surprisingly, the conversation flowed easily when we started talking about baseball and older players from back in the day. She talked about her family and her grandmother always cheating during spades.

"It's beautiful, Gage." She placed her bags down on the bed, as the housekeeper set up lunch.

"For our first adventure, I want to take a walk on the beach and then we will have lunch."

She looked shocked at my statement. That was the problem with Nina Mitchell, she thought she knew everything about me, but I wouldn't let our first meetings be the lasting impression she had of me.

Admiring her beauty, I reached my hand out for her to take, and she smiled, placing her hand in mine, and I led her out to the deck that went toward the beach.

"Do you need a jacket or anything? It can get breezy around this time."

"I got you to keep me warm, I think I'll be fine. So, let's see what this island has to offer." Nina stood on her tiptoes and kissed me on the cheek.

"What's that for?"

"Just wanted to thank you for the trip, even though this happened under weird circumstances."

I leaned down to whisper in her ear, "I plan on showing you that Gage the asshole, can be a lot of fun."

We walked alongside the beach picking up seashells and talked about the history of the island. I brought Li'l Bit here often, and she loved exploring the different caves. The next day, we went fishing and she caught more than I did, of course. She wasn't too humble to brag about catching the most, and her red two-piece bikini had me distracted as it held all her assets just right.

"What are you staring at?" Nina asked taking the captured fish off the hook.

"You," I replied, licking my lips.

"You keep focusing on me and you'll end up never catching anything. I have four to your one in my bucket. What type of bait are you using?"

"Shit, I don't know, something the locals use. Maybe you put a curse on me or something because I seem to not win at anything when you're around," I said morosely.

She giggled at my gloomy expression with my bottom lip tucked between my teeth.

"That's what I've been trying to tell you all along. I'm the best, baby," she said laughing and popping her collar in a funny gesture and I grinned mischievously rubbing my hands together.

"Oh, no. Get that look out of your head right now, Gage."

"Too late, babydoll." I reached out and grabbed her toward me and dunked us both in the ocean.

"Gage! My hair!" Nina screamed, splashing me with water as I laughed at her.

* * *

Two days later we'd laughed, talked, and goofed around like little kids with chucking seashells out to sea. I'd arranged to have privacy and the personal chef made the food and left it for me to serve. Rose petals trailed from the front entrance down the walkway. Low old school Marvin Gaye played in the background; one of the things we discovered that we had in common was we both loved older R&B music.

Nina stood in front of me wearing a see-through dress with a light blue lingerie set before slowly letting her dress fall to the ground. I took a sharp breath at the stunning beauty in front of me. Standing up, I took my time, walking around and taking in every inch of her exquisite body in her panty set. The thong had her ass looking plump and sexy. I could hear her breath hitch as I eased in closer to her sculpted body. This was the moment I'd been waiting for—to make her mine after months of playing cat-and-mouse. I ran a hand over her arm, kissing the back of her neck as she shivered, leaning against my chest. I took a second to walk around glancing up and down her body, etching in my memory every curve and toned muscle that had me wanting to keep her to myself and away from prying eyes. Nina knew what she was doing to me as she stood with a small smirk across her face.

"Damn, you're sexy as fuck."

"Why did you bring me here, Gage?" She moved in close, circling her arms around my neck.

I ran a hand down her soft, smooth back, then down to her ass, grasping a handful, then smacking, and squeezing it as she taunted me. I bet she thought we'd have sex tonight, but it was more about getting to know each other, so her plan of having sex to get rid of me wouldn't work.

"I won the bid at the auction remember?"

"I recall you overbid at the fundraiser and paid five-hundred thousand dollars to keep me from going out on a date with another guy."

"I did. Now put your dress back on."

"What?"

"Nina, I'm not sleeping with you tonight. I want to talk," I answered, pouring a little champagne in each of our glasses and passing her one.

"What if I want to have sex?"

"No."

"No?" she shouted.

"Because you're expecting sex, thinking it would get me to leave you alone, and that's the farthest thing from the truth. I like you. You challenge me."

Her mouth hung open in shock. I winked and pointed to the chair for her to sit down.

"Wait, so you paid all this money to fly me out of the country, just to have dinner and talk?"

"That's not all we'll do."

"So you're telling me you haven't had any sexual thoughts about me since we've been here?" She narrowed her eyes waiting for an answer.

"I didn't say that. You want any of the tilapia?" I pointed toward the plate of food.

"Food is the last thing on your mind. I could see it in your eyes when I wore the red bikini when we went fishing, or when you came to my place and I had on those little bitty shorts and a tank top without a bra. Go ahead and admit that you've been rubbing one out every night since we've been here," she said enticingly, and I almost choked on the champagne. How did she know I ran to the bathroom after fishing the other day because my dick was acting up from being up close to her body, and smelling the coconut scented lotion she applied before we left?

"If I were to admit something like that, then you'd have to admit that you were awake at the same time."

"I'm not afraid to admit I was awake, because of your loud moans," Nina responded moving in closer to me running a hand up and down my chest.

"If I recall, you brought your vibrator here. Where is it?"

The smile dropped from her face. "You just said no

sex," Nina reminded me of my earlier words, rolling her eyes.

"Our rooms are next to each other, Nina. So just like you heard me, I heard you as well, babydoll. We should stop playing games and keep it real with each other," I explained.

"Okay, I want you," she softly muttered.

"Show me," I challenged and she moved in close and wrapped her arms around my neck. Gripping her hips, our lips smashed together as our tongues became familiar with each other.

I flung all the dishes off the table and put her on top of it. The chef had made a nice tilapia with garlic potatoes, salad, and dessert, but the only sweetness I needed was between her thighs.

The urge to bury myself in her slick wetness, caused me to lean her back on top of the table. We continued making out for the rest of the time, with our hands fondling each other.

"Gage, hold up!" Nina moaned as I slid a finger into her wetness.

"Nah, you wanted this, babydoll."

"Gage...please." Nina bit her bottom lip, gripping my shoulders as I pushed her legs farther apart.

That kiss only stirred my appetite for the tantalizing Miss Mitchell. Once the back-and-forth ended, I knew she would see things my way.

Flattening my tongue, I plunged in and out of her sweet core. She trembled in my arms.

"Keep going! Don't stop!" Nina hissed, hitting the top of the table. "Did you bring it?" I said easing another finger inside.

"Bring what, baby?"

I grinned, hearing the nervousness in her voice.

"What did you call him? Billy, Bobby something? I feel like he's family after we've met twice now," I joked about her vibrator that always seemed to make an appearance.

"Mm-hm... mm..." Nina grasped a handful of my hair, pushing my mouth in deeper between her thighs to shut me up.

My erection was raging to be let out and feel her warmth. In order for us to move in the right direction after this trip, we would not be sleeping together.

Chapter Fifteen

Gage

We had been back from the trip for about a week, and things were going great with Nina and I. Yes, it was a little weird buying a date with her, but I knew the only way to get her to agree to dinner was to do something she wouldn't expect. Today I was meeting with the Talbot, Genesis and Jackson, because Talbot wanted to see about me doing an endorsement deal for the bike painting shop. I was early as usual sitting at a corner table at Jane's Restaurant, a nice little bistro that served a variety of foods. I was turned on to shop from Jackson and some of my other teammates, and now everyone wanted to go to his shop. I saw Scottie, right alongside Genesis and Talbot, walking up to the table and Jackson's wife Emery.

"What's that big grin on your face about?" Scottie asked poking me in the side of my rib.

"Scottie, please don't start," I pouted attempting to pull out her chair and Genesis held a hand up that he had it. They were the go to couple for all of our friends. That reminded me that I needed to send flowers to Nina once I left here.

"Gage, don't pout, it doesn't look cute on you. Anyway, I'm starving and you're paying for our lunch," Scottie dictated and Genesis shrugged his shoulders, and Talbot rubbed his hands together mischievously.

"How was the trip, bro? Diya and Scottie have kept me up every night talking on the phone to Nina about Fiji."

You're putting us all to shame with this extra attention," Jackson said.

The server came over and placed menus down for us to look over along with a tray of water. I had the afternoon off today, so it was more of catching up with friends. "Hello, I'm Wendy, I'll be your server today and I have to say, Mr. Young, I'm a huge fan," Wendy said, excitedly.

Seeing her bright smile, I picked up the paper napkin and grabbed her pen out of her hand to sign an autograph. I never tried to deny my fans either a photo or autograph.

"Fiji was great, we went snorkeling, hiking, shopping, and got to know each other better."

Emery picked up her glass of water and took a sip, before saying, "Don't hurt my friend, Gage. I know you player types."

"Babe, let the man figure things out on his own. That relationship has nothing to do with you. Remember how people tried to interfere and ended things under lies." Jackson reminded her and she looked off gesturing for the waitress to come back over.

"Before this lunch goes south with talk of the past, Gage, I wanted to talk to you about endorsing the shop. You know I'm in the process of opening another one up, and I think this would be the perfect time to have a bigger platform for showcasing my business," Talbot explained.

"I can talk to Marcus and a few other guys if you want. I have a few contacts in football and basketball," I replied.

The waitress walked back over and Scottie closed her menu passing it back to her, ready to order.

"Are we all ready to order?" Wendy asked.

"Yes, I will have a turkey club sandwich and salad. Genesis, what are you having?"

"Probably a roast beef sandwich and fries."

"That sounds good actually, maybe I should get that instead," Scottie said, mumbling to herself about the meal she ordered.

"Let me get the same thing as him, except with a root beer to drink," Talbot spoke up.

Talbot and Genesis passed their menus over and I ordered the same thing. "I'll just have a piece of your sandwich and fries, babe," Scottie mentioned, finally coming to a decision on her order.

"Why don't you just order your own?" Genesis questioned.

"Because I can have mine and yours. It's the best part about being a woman. I can have it all," Scottie snickered, leaning over to kiss him on the cheek.

We all laughed and continued on with our lunch, and discussed the shop opening, Celine's time on the softball team with Tailynn, and Genesis's work at the office. These were the moments I appreciated having friends that understood my world and knew the sacrifices it took.

Chapter Sixteen

Nina

We had been back from Fiji for a week now. I was hanging with Diya over at my parents' house. They'd asked me over to discuss the auction and what happened on my trip. I didn't go into too many details, but I let them know some things.

"So, you had fun, sugar?" my grandfather asked.

"I did," I answered, standing to get ready to head out to get my nails done with Diya.

"Mrs. Mitchell, this crumb cake is delicious," Diya stated wiping her mouth as my mom smiled.

"Thank you, sweetie, you want to take some home to Talbot? That boy is too skinny for his own good. You need to bring him over here for Sunday dinner one day, Nina, and let us fatten him up some."

"I like Talbot, he's so cute with all those tattoos. Diya, are y'all married?" my grandmother questioned.

Diya almost choked on her piece of cake, and I groaned in embarrassment. This woman was a mess with her flirting. "Grandma, you can't just ask someone that," I chastised.

"It's fine, NiNi. Ma'am, I'm sorry but Talbot is very much spoken for, we've been married for a while now," Diya responded.

"Well make sure you're cooking some real meals for him, and not that vegan mess that Nina tries to get us to eat," Granny spat rolling her eyes.

"Sorry I'm trying to keep you healthy, woman."

"Anyway, how was the trip?" Mom inquired.

"It was fun, we did a lot of talking, sightseeing, and went out to dinner. The food was incredible. One day we should all go as a family."

Granny butted into the conversation, "And the sex?"

"Grandma!" I screeched in annoyance.

"Child, we're all grown here and your grandfather ain't paying me any mind."

"She's right about that, Nina. Tell us, did Gage put it down or what?" Diya sat back down at the dining room table.

"I'm not having a discussion about my sex life with my grandmother and mother. Now we have a nail appointment, and I have a meeting tonight."

"Meeting for what?" Diya stood up and picked up her purse out of my hands.

"Nothing, important." I grasped her hand leading her out of the dining room to head out to the nail shop.

* * *

His tongue eased inside to meet mine as he glided a rough palm across my abdomen. A chill crept up my body as we entwined our fingers. He lifted my hand and kissed my palm. I gasped, grabbing a fistful of his hair as he trailed kisses down my thigh. I was flooded with memories of our time in Fiji, on a secluded island, and him making me feel things that I didn't want to admit I felt.

"Gage, don't tease me." I drew in a frustrated breath. He knew what he was doing, and this was our first time, and I expected that he wanted it to last as long as possible.

"Baby, you are fucking beautiful. Damn... I'm a lucky man." A low groan left his lips.

A bolt of desire moved through my body. He intoxicated me like a fine liquor, tingles bounded up my arm.

We couldn't even make it up to my room. The dinner tonight with some of his teammates and friends was amazing and it let me know that he's serious about getting to know me, and pursuing more than just a sexual relationship.

"Shit! Mmmm..." I hissed from the prolonged anticipation as his lips became familiar with every inch of my pussy, and then moved back up toward my breasts. My left nipple leapt to attention against his tongue. He trailed his fingers down my stomach and into my wet curls. I knew some men wanted a woman completely shaven, but based on our time in Fiji, I could tell that Gage liked a little stubble. My nipples beaded under his scrutiny.

"I can't promise I won't bury myself so deep in you that I'll forget to take it easy on you, babydoll. You're everything I wanted, hoped, and ever dreamed about," Gage said desperately.

"No more talking, Gage." I shuddered under his touch.

I didn't think we would make it this far because after the auction, I wanted nothing to do with him. He was not only a famous athlete, and a father to one of the kids I coached, but Gage could also be an asshole, arrogant, and cocky more than anything. Dealing with a man who wouldn't understand that he wasn't the center of my world could spell trouble. During the amount of time we had spent together since the auction and our trip showed that Gage was more determined to prove to me that striking a balance and compromise was something that he could bring to my life. It didn't hurt that I loved his daughter, Tailynn, and I had even become friends with his ex-girlfriend and the mother of his daughter.

He leaned back and smiled. I reached out to touch his taut, muscular chest, letting my hand glide all the way down to the opening of his boxers that showcased a few curls that covered his thick dick. I'd felt it many times but never saw it before. He looked about eight inches or more. I closed my eyes and inhaled all the air I could as he helped guide my hand into his boxers to stroke his girth. A raw, primitive groan overwhelmed him. His head flung back in pleasure. Every time his gaze met mine, my heart turned over in response.

"I want you, Gage," I said, my eyes raking over his body boldly.

He was as eager and erratic as a summer storm. Something in his manner soothed me at the same time. Grabbing the condom out of his pants pockets he passed it to me to sheath him. Watching as I rolled the condom down, his steady gaze fell to the creamy expanse of my pussy. Licking his lips, he lifted my left leg trailing kisses from the palm of my foot, biting and nipping at my leg as he sunk his large girth within my folds.

"Let me feel you, Gage!" I cried out in ecstasy, hooking my left leg around his waist and gripping his sides as he started to thrust in and out.

"Baby, I apologize for being selfish," Gage groaned

into my hair, lowering his lips, and biting my shoulder as his thrusts sped up.

"Apologize for what, baby?" I moaned, wrapping my arms around his neck. I lifted my hips, meeting him thrust for thrust.

He lowered his head and brushed kisses across my jaw, cheek, and lips. I brushed a thumb across his soft, pillowy bottom lip. "This feels like home," Gage sighed, pushing my legs wider as our groans and grunts echoed throughout the living room.

"Ugh, God! Yes... right there." I couldn't hold out any longer as sweat trailed down my chest.

Gage teased my lips apart and swept his tongue into my mouth, shifting the kiss from persuasive to demanding. He clasped his strong arms around me, pumping faster and faster. Then, he abruptly pulled out, smacking, and soothing my ass before my orgasm erupted.

"Gage!" I screamed, trying to grip his thick girth, and put him back inside.

He smacked my hand away, and I whimpered, shifting my angle toward him so he could slip it back in, as our juices melded together. The mere touch of his hand sent a warming shiver through me. I lifted my ass in the air, facing the wall and making a perfect arch. His hands locked around my waist and he planted himself again. We both groaned at the same time. His thrusts grew wilder, and his hands caressed the planes of my back. He engulfed me in comfort. As his thrusts grew in speed, I moved my hand to my clit, rubbing harder and harder, as both of our all-consuming orgasms neared.

"Oh, shit!" Gage yelled, tightening his grip, his large body covering my back, his lips biting and licking my back. "Turn over; I want to taste you, babydoll," Gage said.

Turning my head, I met his lips with a kiss. "You feel so good, Gage," I moaned into his mouth. Our tongues battled to be on top.

"You do too, baby."

"Fuck!" We both moaned at the same time as we both came, falling onto the hard carpet with his weight on top of my body, and our breathing in sync. He rolled off my back and pulled me into his arms, kissing my forehead and encircling me like a cocoon as we drifted off to sleep.

"Your soft hands feel so good on me, baby," Gage whispered.

* * *

Today, Gage surprised me with a date to the local softball field. This was our first real official date if you didn't count him bidding on me at the auction. I wiped the sweat off my brow as he stood behind me to make sure I had the perfect posture.

"Gage, have you forgotten that I played ball professionally?"

"I know, but you can always improve."

I dropped the bat and turned to glare as his lips turned up into a smirk—the same lips that had my pussy tingling, and me screaming for mercy last night. "Have you always been like this?" I continued, pretending to swing the bat as the machine geared up to spit out a few balls at lightning speed.

"What? Confident?"

"Confident or cocky, arrogant, asshole..." He raised his hand cutting me off from continuing.

"Aren't we here for you to learn a few tricks? I remember you were the one who lost the bet, my dear."

"For me to lose a bet, I would have had to participate in one wholeheartedly."

"So, are you saying you lost on purpose, in fact letting me think I won? So, in turn, I would have to one day return the favor?"

"That brain of yours is really working overtime, huh? Does your ego leave any room for humbleness, Mr. Young?"

"Gage."

"I like Mr. Young."

He moved in closer. "I like Daddy."

"Then you should call Tailynn up because she's the only person who'll be calling you 'Daddy,' Mr. Young," I said, then hitting one, two, and three balls back-to-back.

Chapter Seventeen

Nina

I buttoned up my jeans, and checked my pockets to make sure that I had my keys, and grabbed my jacket from my closet. I was meeting my dad, and a few of the girls from the softball team at the game. Gage invited me along with my friends and family. Picking up my hairbrush, I swooped my hair up into a bun, and popped on my favorite clear lip-gloss. Nicole was coming along to the game as moral support, and to help manage the girls.

"How do I look?" Nicole asked, stepping further into my room with a short romper and tank top, with knee boots on.

"Where's the rest of your clothes?"

"What's wrong with this?'

She could not be serious in wanting to go out half dressed, and to a game in an outfit that barely covered her ass. I arched a skeptical brow.

"Nicole, are you going to a baseball game or to the club? Sometimes I wonder if Mom and Dad adopted you."

"Who's playing today anyway?"

Grabbing my sunglasses, she followed behind me out of my condo as I locked up. I saw a message from Samantha that she was meeting me there with Tailynn and Kaylee. Then another message popped up from Scottie, letting us all know that she was bringing Celine.

I replied back to everyone that I'd see them soon. Nicole turned the radio up as we pulled out of the parking garage.

"So, Mister Loverboy lives in the same building as you?"

"Yep. Will you text Dad and see if he's on his way yet? I got the tickets so he needs to meet us up front at the gate." I quickly changed lanes to get on the freeway as I listened to Nicole talking to our father about what area to meet us at once he arrived at the stadium. This was our way of keeping his spirits up while we look for alternatives for moving the center if our injunction didn't hold.

The stadium was packed with the large screens showing the home team New York Raptors vs. Los Angeles Devils. I wasn't sure if Gage was playing today, and hanging out with his daughter outside of practice was always a good time.

"What does Emery think of you guys dating?" Nicole stated, firing off another text message.

"She loves it, because their kids and Tailynn are friends. Plus, Jackson, Genesis and Gage run in the same circles. This is the first time I've ever dated anyone with a child, so I'm trying to be respectful of her time with him and not make it as though he's with me more than her, if that makes any sense."

She nodded in agreement.

"I can see how that could be an issue. But you even

said that you get along with Samantha, and she's engaged to someone else and Tailynn loves him."

We showed our VIP badges that Gage left at my place. We left a badge for my dad with the security guard while another escort from the stadium walked us over to our seats as we waited for everyone else to arrive.

"Samantha is great, and she invited me with them on their weekly outings to the spa and it's become like a girl's thing now. Tailynn is spoiled and a Daddy's girl, kind of like you."

"There he is, with security." Nicole waved over my shoulder and I saw my dad, towering above the shorter statured security guard.

He came through the crowd and hugged us both, and sat in the middle of us like always.

"These are great seats, Nina." My father clapped and cheered as the announcer started to announce the starting lineup.

"Nicole and I wanted to do something fun with you to take your mind off of things," I said just as Nicole stood up.

"I'm going to grab something to eat, and then walk around a little, there are a lot of cute guys in here." Nicole popped her booty, pretending to twerk a little in the stands. My dad rolled his eyes in embarrassment.

"What about the game?"

"It's not going anywhere. I'll be back, and there's Samantha, Scottie, and the girls."

Scottie allowed Celine and Tailynn to walk in front of them, and she sat beside me. As we continued talking and watching the game, I knew that Nicole would find her way back to us at some point. My dad talked with Tailynn and Samantha as the game started, and I pulled out my phone and texted Gage.

Me: *Good luck today.*

Gage: *Enjoy yourself.*

"These seats are nice, NiNi," Scottie commented, passing me a bag of popcorn.

"Thanks, boo. Celine, aren't you looking like a diva today?"

Celine waved at me and sat next to Tailynn, then they pulled out their phones and commenced to taking selfies.

"Were we like them at their age?" Scottie questioned with a wide grin.

Nodding in agreement, I passed the popcorn over to Tailynn. "Where did Nicole go?" Scottie asked looking around.

"You know her, there really is no telling where she's at, anyway how was your day? We haven't caught up since I arrived back home."

"Because someone's been holding you hostage from your friends."

"Now who would that be? Because if I recall right, he's your friend as well." I motioned over to the kids laughing to show the foundation of the relationship between Gage, Genesis, and Talbot.

"We did."

"I can see the glow on your face, girl. Just remember to breathe through your nose," Scottie joked, and we clapped hands.

"Oh my God! You're a mess. I'm so over you. How does Genesis put up with you all the time?" I asked nudging her in the arm.

"Easily, with me breathing through my nose I can get away with almost anything."

We burst out in laughter and continued watching the game.

"Okay, you win this round. Anyway, we had lunch a couple of days ago and he said you guys had a great time."

Chapter Eighteen

Nina

"Nina, you slept with Gage Young? What was it like? I need all the details," Maya insisted, turning the channel off.

I'd invited her, Nicole, Samantha, and Diya over for takeout and wine. Scottie couldn't make it because of work. She was probably the one I needed the most advice from, since she'd dealt with the same situation with her husband, whom she hated at first, but ended falling in love and having a kid with.

Yes, Gage was gorgeous, but the cockiness was too much to handle. I found myself wanting to smack him whenever he gave me that little smirk. The problem was, if I stared into his eyes long enough, I had no choice but to agree with whatever he wanted.

"I don't know what I was thinking, you guys. He's so not my type."

"What, rich and sexy?" Maya asserted, pointing to the gossip magazine with a photo of Gage on the cover. The doorbell rang and I stood up, walking over to look out of the peephole and saw Samantha and Diya together.

"NiNi, you have a secret admirer." Samantha pointed to the delivery man standing behind her, holding a massive bouquet of white roses in his hands.

I reached out to sign the clipboard and grabbed the flowers. I thanked him and took the card out. *The memory of your sweet taste on my lips still lingers. I can't wait to feel you again, babydoll,* the card read.

"Nina, you got that man so whipped," Nicole jested, taking the flowers out of my hand, and smelling them.

"Let's not talk about my sex life, okay?"

The next morning, Romi picked me up and we drove over to the bank to have a meeting with a loan officer about a possible extension on our loan. The money from the auction would only hold us over for a few more weeks. Most, if not all the businesses surrounding us had already closed up shop because this real estate company let the property sit and raise prices to where no one could move in that lived on a certain level of fixed income. Especially if you thought of working in the same area you lived. Jobs weren't paying like they used to, like back when my parents were young.

Chapter Nineteen

Gage

Practice finished early, and my brother texted me to meet at the office to deal with the little problem of the company buying up more land. A blush crept over his secretary's face as I walked in. Anna always had a crush on me, and since we were the same age, she often flirted. I can't lie and say I didn't sleep with her, but once we hooked up, she became too attached, and I wasn't ready to settle down, at least not with her.

"Gage, nice to see you again. I was hoping we could talk after your meeting?" Anna begged, leaning over her desk, and adjusting her bra to show off her large breasts. Her mission was to marry into the family, and since Daniel already had a wife and kids, her intention was to seduce me into bringing her to various family functions.

I was called into a meeting with my father to go over the expansion of the business. Currently, I've been stressed with not only our upcoming game, but also keeping the secret to myself.

"Anna, you know it's never going to happen again.

You're too clingy, baby. Plus, you bragged to everyone in the office about us sleeping together."

"I never told anyone. I promise, Gage, give me another chance."

"Sorry, but it's too close to home."

"Because I work for your family?"

"Amongst other things," I sighed, leaving to go deal with my family.

Pushing the massive door open I stepped inside with both of my brothers, my father, and his long-time banker.

"Ethan West." We've butted heads a few times in passing. He was thinking of running for governor or president. His ego is just as big as my father's. It didn't help that we went to college together. He came from money as well, and invested in different businesses and on his own became a billionaire by the age of twenty-eight.

"Gage, good to see you."

"Wish I could say the same, Ethan."

"Ouch, are you still having hurt feelings from your ex wanting to sleep with me?"

"Samantha told me you guys went out on one date, and we were broken up at the time, so I have no hard feelings about you besides your overinflated ego."

"Gentlemen, as entertaining as this whole conversation is, I didn't call you both here for a pissing match," my father commanded as he stood from his seat.

"Good, because he wouldn't win, unless he tried some sneaky underhanded shit like you to get ahead."

"Testy I see."

"Man, why am I here?"

"You're here because we have a few more buildings we need you to go to with your brother to have a look around, and Ethan is thinking of running for office. It would be great to get in on the ground floor and for our business to be attached to his campaign."

Groaning, I jumped up, getting ready to walk out of this meeting, until Gordon called my name.

"Come on, Gage, I'm the first person to tell you when Dad's a jackass," my brother spoke.

"Gordon, watch your mouth," our father chastised.

"Forget about what he's saying, this is one way to make sure your girl can get her place back before it's sold off."

"That's not a part of this conversation," I reminded them.

"Ohh, I heard about the little softball coach and her family's community center going under. Does she know about your little interview with that celebrity gossip chick?" Ethan asked snidely.

He stood off to the side with a smug grin across his face.

"Shut the fuck up," I snapped, charging toward him when Gordon jumped in front of me.

I smoothed my hand down my face trying to calm down. For Ethan to know about Nina, pissed me off which means either my father or my brother was talking about me behind my back. I arched a knowing brow.

"Tobias, I'll be in touch. Gage, it was nice seeing you again, please tell Samantha I said hello," Ethan said.

Before I could continue, I received a text with the flight information for our out of town game. Replying with a yes confirmation, I closed out of the message and placed my phone back in my pocket.

"I need to go, I have a game and this little intervention, or whatever the hell you call it, is the last thing on my mind," I emphasized, shaking hands with Gordon, and purposefully ignoring everyone else in the room. Glancing around the room, I shook my head and opened the door. I left out my father, not caring if I spoke to him again.

Once the Nationals are done, I'll work on figuring out a way to help Nina's family somehow. He may have people in high places, pulling the strings, but one thing I've learned is that he needs me more than I need him.

Chapter Twenty

Gage

"**W**hy not come out to the game and watch me play?"

"I'm busy with my family, besides you don't need me to cheer you on, you have your fans going crazy over you and wanting your undivided attention," Nina responded, giggling through the phone. She'd sent a photo of me from the blogs, it was of me with some women from another game and I was annoyed she wasn't here to keep my mind straight. I found myself missing her more and more. Even sleeping at night, I wanted her by my side.

"A quick flight won't hurt, and forget about the blogs, babydoll. You know that stuff's all fake."

"Well, I'm still not coming. I have a lot to handle here, and you'd probably be more into your game than worrying about hanging with me."

"I never get tired of having you around."

"Have you talked to Tailynn yet?" she asked, effectively changing the subject.

"Soon as I hang up with you, I'm calling her. Don't try

and change the subject either. I can have a jet sent for you within an hour."

"Gage."

"I'm not trying to force my money on you, I just miss having you next to me."

"I miss you too. But call your daughter and get your head in the game," she said hanging up the phone.

A few minutes later, I was FaceTiming with Tailynn. This was our nightly ritual we'd started a few years back when she stayed with her mother or even while I was out of town at away games. We'd talk about her day and my day, then delve into our secret handshake of slapping hands three times, turning around and slapping hands again. Since she wasn't here, we had to fake it through FaceTime.

"I think I'm dizzy, Daddy." She lifted her eyes, swaying side to side. I wanted to laugh at her, but I knew she'd be embarrassed.

"Li'l Bit, sit down before you fall down. Did you finish your homework? You know your mom won't let you watch TV until you do."

"Yep, and she checked over everything so I can watch the game on time and not miss you. I told Celine and Kaylee to call me so we can all watch together." Nodding at her comment, I was reminded that I needed to hit up Genesis about the situation with Nina's family and possibly get some advice on how to rectify the situation and keep Nina in my life.

"I have to get going, baby, I love you and tell your mom I said hi. I'm walking into the locker room now."

"Bye, Daddy! Knock him out!" she said excitedly.

"Thanks, baby."

I hung up with my baby and closed the door of the

locker room. The entire team stood in line ready to head out on the field as everyone stayed silent, and gathered their thoughts before walking out with a few security personnel. Marcus and I continued talking as the announcer was starting the game.

"You ready for this, G?" Marcus commented, kissing his favorite good luck charm, a quarter that his father gave him his first time playing in the game when he was younger. Now that his dad was no longer living, he kept that quarter in his pocket for every game.

"Always."

* * *

"Ladies and gentlemen, welcome to the plate the one and only Gage Young, a four-time MVP, Rookie of the Year winner, and two-time World Series champion," the announcer's voice came over the speakers, bolstered by the loud roaring of the fans as they stood and cheered.

Tipping my hat at the dedicated response, I wanted to make sure we brought the crowd a good game.

Running onto the field and over to the dugout, we listened to the coach call out the first plays and looked to the stands at all of the fans cheering and waving.

* * *

After winning our away game, I came back to my hotel room to relax. The guys wanted me to go out and hit up a few bars, but I wasn't feeling that social. I missed not only Li'l Bit, but also my babydoll. Waving to the night desk clerk, I jumped on the elevator and rode up to my penthouse suite. I'd paid out of pocket to upgrade my room for privacy, since a few of my single teammates made it a habit of bringing girls back to their rooms when we were on the road, and rooming with another one of the guys was out of the question for me. Pushing my keycard inside the slot, I walked through the door and dropped my bags on the floor. I was exhausted from the game, and all I wanted to do was shower and sleep the night away.

Hopefully Nina was still awake. Having her with me for support during an away game was something I'd dreamed about. Heading into my bedroom, I pulled my shirt off and gasped, seeing Nina standing in front of my bed, wearing the sexiest lingerie that covered every curve.

"What are you doing here, babydoll?"

"I wanted to surprise you."

Dropping my shirt on the floor, I unbuckled my pants and kicked my shoes off.

She smirked, heading toward me. I slid the gown off her shoulders and down her arms. Taking her hand, I guided it to my hard dick. I was salivating. She looked like an angel before me, and I didn't want her to ever be away from me. Her pink nipples hardened at my touch. She slowly kissed downward, skimming my thighs. The pleasure was pure and explosive. I knew she wanted to be in control, but a part of me wouldn't last long if she continued on this current trajectory. The warmth of her soft flesh was intoxicating. Anything she wanted from me, I would give her in a heartbeat.

Gently easing her down onto the bed, she surprised me by flipping us over with her on top.

"I see what type of party you're on tonight, babydoll."

"What type, Mr. Young?" she teased, winding her hips on top of my lap. I could feel the heat from her pussy. She wasn't wearing any underwear.

"Did anybody see you in this?" I asked, pointing to her nightgown on the floor.

She shook her head and leaned over to kiss my lips. She took my index finger, tracing it across her lips, and then sliding it into her mouth, pretending she was sucking my dick. One hand slid down her taut stomach to the swell of her hips.

"No, I changed when I got in the room. I talked to Marcus and he told me what room you were staying in, he's the biggest flirt in the world and the front desk clerk is excited about going on a date with him, so he told me you owe him big time, because he now has to take her on a very expensive date to make up for getting a key to your room. He explained that he left some of his bags in your room in order to get the key to come inside, and I came up with him and then changed after he left."

"Damn you look sexy, baby."

"Only for you, Mr. Young," she teased.

Hearing her say "Mr. Young" only made me want to fuck her even harder. Shifting her angle I slid inside of her, it was tight and wet, and her face was flushed with satisfaction. She pressed her breasts against my chest as she squeezed my dick in a chokehold inside of her pussy. I needed to think of something else before I came too quickly.

"Fuck! You're trying to cause me to go to jail, baby-doll," I growled.

"Why do you sa...Ughhh...Gage!"

I drove into her, thrusting as the headboard started to rock against the wall. I didn't care if other guests reported us or not. We'd be making love all throughout the night and day. She cooed, reaching up to clasp the back of my head to pull me down for a kiss. I gripped both sides of her ass, squeezing as I deepened the kiss.

"Mhmmm...Shit!" I moaned, tightening my grip on her thighs. Some men hated to moan during sex. When it was feeling good, I wanted my woman to know she was making me feel good, same as if I was pleasing to her. Leaning down I bit her bottom lip and our moans grew louder.

"Yes! G...Gagggge!"

Chapter Twenty-One

Nina

Standing in the shower, I watched as Gage continued his so-called "singing," to Brian McKnight's "The One". The defined muscles in his back undulated as the water ran down his back in rivulets. The things he had done to my body, put all my past lovers to shame. He had the ability to make my body feel out of this world. But I had to push him back, and keep him from getting too close to me. I wasn't ready for the constant media attention, and the groupies constantly trying to get in the middle.

"Come here, babydoll," Gage demanded, grasping his thick length, and biting his bottom lip suggestively.

Shaking my head, I walked out of the bathroom as he followed, turned the water off, and grabbed a towel. I turned away, going back into the living room of the suite. We had one day out here in Philly, so we had planned to sightsee before driving back to New York. He had a few days before the Nationals, so he was determined to spend every moment with Tailynn and me. It was funny to see us now, compared to how we started as enemies constantly running into each other, and then how he tried to take over coaching my softball team.

"Gage, we only have one day here, aren't you tired from the multiple rounds we had last night?"

"Nope, that pretty little pussy of yours keeps me energized."

"As flattering as I think your comment is meant to be, I need a break. We have a day full of fun planned, so get dressed and meet me in the living room," I said, running over to my luggage to grab a pair of jeans and t-shirt to get dressed for the day.

He walked over with a towel wrapped around his waist and hugged me from behind, stopping me from pulling up my pants with a strong grasp on my pussy. He wiggled a finger inside as I muttered unintelligible words under my breath.

"This isn't fair."

He ran his tongue across my shoulder. I tilted my head to the side as he nipped and bit my neck. Shimmering arousal was thrumming in my core. "Okay, just one more round, and then we head out for the day."

* * *

The crisp autumn air and the bright sunshine made for the perfect day to shop, have lunch, and see a show or two. The team had security follow alongside us as we spent the day roaming the city. Normally, I could have handled myself alone, but since he wanted to be extra cautious with me, I didn't put up a fight.

We stopped off at a local sports bar for lunch. The

loud, fifty-two inch TVs aired all kinds of sports, from basketball, to football, to a recap of Gage's team's latest win. I clapped, whistled, and cheered for my man as we shared a Philly cheesesteak and beers. The waitress brought out another basket of fries as security stood off to the right side of our booth, keeping fans away.

"Why'd you stop playing, if you don't mind me asking?" Gage probed.

I took a swig of beer while thinking of an answer. I wiped my mouth with my napkin and took another french fry out of his basket. The man could eat anyone out of house and home. "I wanted to retire before I really injured myself. Plus, I was spending more time at my family's business," I explained, and watched as a look of concern marred his face.

"Yeah, I can understand wanting to leave while you were still mobile. You think your girls will go toward the championship?" Gage asked.

He changed the subject. I picked up on the sudden change in his mood when it came to my family. I knew he has struggled with his family's dealings judging by what he has told me in the past about how they were wanting him to go into the real estate business.

"I think we have a good chance if we continue practicing. What has you so distracted though? I watched your game the other night and you seemed off. And when we made love last night, you seemed more possessive than usual, Mr. Young."

He picked up his beer and took a sip, trying to buy himself some time to respond.

"What would you do if someone broke your trust?"

"It depends on the situation, but I would more than

likely stop talking to them, why? You have something to confess?"

"I know the money didn't completely help with covering the expenses for your family's community center."

"How do you know that?"

"Listen, babydoll, I know you don't want to hear this, but let me give you the money for the center."

"I'm not with you for your money, Gage."

"Trust me, you've made that abundantly clear."

"Someone's getting a little beside themselves."

"Nina my-"

The waitress walked back over with another beer right as the team security guard bent down and whispered in Gage's ear. He nodded in agreement and checked his phone.

"What's wrong?"

He stood up grasping my chin, kissing me on the lips. I puckered my lips for another kiss. "The coach just texted me about something, I need to make a phone call really quick. Can you order us another basket of ribs? I'm starving."

I took a bite of one of the ribs. I wiped my mouth right as my phone buzzed. Seeing my brother's name flash across the screen, I picked it up and looked at his messages.

Nick: *Yo, I have to tell you something.*

Me: *What are you talking about?*

Nick: *We'll discuss it when you get back.*

Me: *Is it Romi or the baby?*

Nick: *No, they are just fine. Talk when you get back.*

I clicked out of my messages right as Gage walked back to our booth. He kissed my cheek again and I didn't want to end the trip so abruptly, but my family was important to me, and something was definitely up at home.

Chapter Twenty-Two

Gage

"**O**h, my God! Look at Maya! She's doing her thang! The caption says she has an exclusive report! Tell the waitress to turn the volume up!"

I waved the waitress over and asked if she could turn the volume up a little more. The crowd seemed to die down as the speakers blared; Maya was talking and holding a piece of paper.

"Hello, my loves. You know me; I'm all about the truth and keeping you informed. So, what I'm about to say is very hard for me, but I need to keep it one-hundred percent with you always—even when it includes someone whom I know very well."

An eerie feeling crept into my stomach. I felt like whatever bomb she was going to drop had something to do with Nina and me. "Babe, let's get out of here and go catch that movie you wanted to see." I tried to slip out of the booth and placed some money on the table.

She waved me off and stared at the screen as a picture

of me and my father was shown, then her family's center. "What the hell?" she whispered under her breath.

"Nina, let's go." I tried to reach for her, but she snatched her hand away from me, shaking her head as her eyes started to well up.

"Loves, this is hot off the presses. From my sources, Gage Young's family just bought the land that houses the Mitchell Community Center. Not only was the money raised to save the property, but somehow it mysteriously went missing, and the property was sold to Young Financial Industries. I'm close to this situation, which is why I'm being very transparent with you. As you may have heard, my best friend is currently dating Mr. Young."

"Tell me it isn't true?" she asked standing up grabbing her purse, pulling out her wallet.

"Nina, let's talk about this back at the hotel. I can explain; your girl isn't telling the truth."

"Did your father purchase my family's property? It's a simple yes or no question, Gage."

My shoulders slumped. There was no way out of this situation, and her look of hurt and betrayal was twisting my stomach into knots. She might think this was the end of us, but I would not let her walk out of my life for good. I stepped forward to gently touch her hand, but she jerked back in pain, as though I had hurt her in a way I could never recover from. "I ..."

"No need to explain. Your silence speaks volumes, Mr. Young. Stay away from me; don't try to contact me, and if Tailynn has practice, please have someone else drop her off. I don't want to end my friendship with Tailynn because of you, but you need to understand that whatever we had between us is over." Nina gestured between me and her, dropped a twenty-dollar bill on the table and walked off.

Security tried to follow her, but she motioned for them to stay back. I nodded at them to do as she requested.

The best thing that had happened to me since the birth of my daughter just walked out of my life, all because of my family's insatiable greed.

* * *

I barged into my father's office. He sat at his desk with a host of his lawyers and accountants gathered around him.

I didn't care about interrupting whatever they had going on. "Get out!" I sneered, walking over to my father's desk. The rest of his employees filtered out—except my brother.

"What's your problem?" he questioned.

"Don't fucking talk to me."

"Gage, you're in my office; show some respect to your brother—*and* my business."

"Fuck your business. I told you to leave the Mitchell property alone, and you go behind my back and pull this bullshit?"

"What are you taking about?"

"I'm talking about the community center. You knew I wanted it to be left alone. You went behind my back and bought it up—or paid someone to forge the documents necessary to steal the property. Fix it now, and then leave them alone."

"Is this about your little girlfriend's family? This is business, Gage; we can't feel sorry for every sad story that comes into play. Our business is buying property, and turning a profit," Daniel nonchalantly stated, sitting back down on the couch and opening a file folder.

I stalked toward him and gripped his neck, just as security burst in and tried to pull me off him.

"Gage, that is enough. We don't let anyone come before family," Father justified, sitting back down at his desk as I jerked out of the security guard's hands.

"Either you give them back their property, or lose your son and granddaughter."

He chuckled at my comment, shaking his head in disappointment that I cared more about Nina, than him and this company.

"Are you threatening me? You *do* realize this would hurt your mother more than me, right?"

"Mom would understand. I refuse to be mixed up in this mess. Have you seen the latest news channels talking about how trashy it seems that I'm living life up with a potentially huge endorsement deal from winning the World Series?" But the Young brand that I've helped to build in the community is tarnished because you want another pot of gold in your pocket."

"That's enough!" he shouted, slamming his hand down on the desk.

"Don't call me and you sure as hell better not use my games to set up meetings to influence your potential clients."

"Gage!"

I turned my back to him and walked out, slamming the door behind me.

Jumping in my car I sped off, dialing Nina's number again.

"This mailbox is full."

"Fuck!"

Hearing that she blocked me for real fucked me up. I knew the one place she'd probably be, and I could try to get her to listen to me.

It didn't take long to arrive at the community center. I saw for lease signs outside as some crew continued cleaning up the field and mowed the lawn. Jumping out of the car and strolling inside, I showed my ID at the front desk.

"Who are you here to see, sir?" the receptionist inquired.

"Is Nina Mitchell working today?"

"She's not in today, is there a message I can take for you?"

"Stalking won't get her back, you know."

I turned at the voice behind me and he seemed familiar.

"Nicholas." Nina's older brother. He extended a hand and I hesitated, wondering if he was testing me to see I was one of those guys that were intimidated by a big brother. "Gage Young." Probably setting me up to slip a closed fist across my jaw.

"I'm not your biggest fan, but I know my sister likes you. So, I won't kick your ass at this moment, even though you and your entire family deserves it."

"I appreciate you taking the time to talk with me. I saw your trophies on the wall in the outside display. Do you miss playing professionally?"

He motioned for me to follow and we headed to his office. "I did, same as Nina playing professional softball. We get our love of sports from my dad, and some say our competitive nature as well. Working here brings us the same sense of accomplishment though."

Stepping aside he held the door as I looked around at all the trophies and posters of him and Nina.

"Wow."

"Nina was bad ass when she played professionally. Have a seat."

"Thanks, but I won't keep you long."

He motioned for me to take a seat in the chair across from his. I couldn't help but notice a picture of him, Nina, and Nicole when they were younger. The smile captured a genuine person that could light up an entire room with her smile, and caused me to never want to hurt her again if I have the chance to make things right.

Clearing his throat, he fixed me with his unrelenting gaze. "I take it Nina kicked your ass to the curb?"

"She told you about my family?"

He stood from his desk and sat on the edge, wearing a hard frown. "I was the one that found out your dad's dummy corporation was behind the LLC of the real estate company that's putting our center out of business. I know you thought pulling off a miracle with the auction would help, but after paying off the back taxes and getting things updated, we still didn't make the final dues. Your family's only after money and I'm not sorry that I warned her about your family."

"What Nina and I have has nothing to do with my father or you. I didn't have anything to do with my father's decision to be money hungry. I offered to donate whatever funds were necessary to keep the center open, but your sister refused to take a dime from me."

"Is that supposed to make me feel sorry for you? Because I don't, we both know if you didn't have an invested interest in my sister, you probably wouldn't have ever batted an eye at this place."

"I didn't come here for a lecture. Yes, I found out later about his involvement and didn't tell Nina because I was afraid she'd leave me. Haven't you ever loved someone and didn't mean to cause them any harm, even though you thought you were protecting them? My daughter is the most important thing to me, and keeping her in a safe and positive environment is my number one focus. She loved playing at the center and making friends with all the kids who come here. Yeah, I noticed the signs of the construction company around the neighborhood whenever I dropped Tailynn off for practice, but I couldn't disappoint her and I never saw Nina and I becoming more. It was a surprise all the way around and if it meant leaving her alone to be happy without me, I would try as long and Tailynn was secure and good."

"No doubt, but you, my friend, fucked up big time." He rose from the edge of his desk and stared out of the window.

"I'm still working on figuring out how to fix this situation."

"Are you fixing it in hopes of getting my sister back, or to actually help the members of the community that come here for support? Most big time celebrities just throw out that they'll help, and you never hear from them again."

"You'll have to take my word that I'll get this fixed, either with Nina or without her."

Chapter Twenty-Three

Gage

A month later, Nina was still ignoring my calls, emails, and only Samantha could drop Tailynn off for practice—and even then, her assistant did most of the coaching. It was like we never even existed. Listening to Marcus and Talbot talk about how I should have been honest with her from the start really wasn't helping matters any. I knew they were right; I had been stubborn and thought that I had more than enough time to fix things before she found out, but that hadn't worked out as planned.

The same day when I stormed into my father's office was the last time I spoke to him or my brother. Even my mother was calling me constantly, and I ignored her questions. Samantha let Tailynn visit with her only at her place because she agreed with me about my family's approach to the entire situation.

"He really looks pitiful. What if we go out and meet some girls? I have a date who could probably hook you up with one of her friends, man," Marcus stated, snapping his fingers in front of my face.

I really felt off-balance and in a daze from no longer seeing or talking to Nina almost every day. "I'm not in the mood."

"Gage, you look like shit and you have Nationals coming up soon. Snap out of whatever this funk is that you're in," Talbot commanded, standing up and walking over to grab his gloves to start creating the tattoo of Nina's name that I wanted drawn over my heart.

"He's looking like a straight up girl that got dumped," Marcus joked, padding over to the other guys in the tattoo shop and laughing and slapping hands.

"Fuck you," I snapped, flipping them both off.

"I'm serious, Gage; you've always been this hardcore, don't-take-any-shit type of dude, and now you have one break-up, and it's the end of the world. Let me hook you up tonight," Marcus said, coming to sit in the chair next to me.

I ran a hand across my face. I hadn't shaved since the Philly game. All my thoughts were on Nina, and what she was doing—and whom she was doing it with.

"Who is she?" I asked, removing my shirt so that Talbot could sketch the outline of Nina's name.

Talbot shook his head and I already knew what he was going to say, but I was determined to distract myself before Tailynn came over later that night. I wasn't planning on having sex or marrying the girl, I was doing a favor for a friend and my mindset was fucked up over Nina so having drinks with a few friends wouldn't hurt.

"This is a bad idea, Gage. Take it from me. You're going through the same situation that I was in with my ex. You can't get over someone by jumping into something else over a misunderstanding. Give her some space, and then talk to her once you've both had a chance to calm down," Talbot begged, finishing the outline of Nina's name in cursive.

"Talbot, you're married, what do you know about the single life?" Marcus interjected.

"I know that stupid shit like this will only end up with Gage hurting Nina even more. But don't take my advice. You'll learn, and by then it'll be too late," Talbot berated him.

The vibration of my phone pulled my attention away, and I took it out of my pants pocket, looking at a picture of Nina half-dressed, out, and hugging up on some guy. I couldn't really tell who it was because of the angle. She wasn't too heartbroken if she was already dating someone new. Shutting my phone off, I stuck it back in my pocket and winced as the tattoo needle pinched a little harder than usual.

"Marcus I'll take you up on that date. Nina apparently isn't worried about me, so I might as well move on as well."

Marcus grinned, fist-bumping me, as Talbot continued with the tattoo before I could stop him. It would just be a memory that I'd wear on my body of a love I once knew.

* * *

"Gage, are you listening to me?" Tiffany whispered in my ear.

Regret hit me soon as I sat down for this date. Tiffany was an assistant of Marcus's agent and she'd asked me out a few times in the past. But so far, the only thing she'd done was babbled on about taking pictures for Genesis. I refused, because I didn't need to be associated with any more social media relationships. If I ever got Nina back, the last thing I wanted her to think was that I was out hooking up with random women.

"Tiffany, I'm sorry, but I need to go, I have an emergency with my daughter," I lied and stood up from the table pulling out two hundred dollars and placing it on the table. Even though we didn't order, I wanted to make up for not finishing our date.

"How old is your daughter? I mean, where's her mother?" Tiffany wrinkled up her nose like she smelled rotten socks.

"She's working. Wait, you don't like kids?"

"Kids like in babies? No, they cry, poop, and fuss all day. I'd rather adopt a teenager, someone self-sufficient. Is your daughter over fifteen?" Tiffany inquired picking up the two hundred dollars and placing it in her bra.

"She's ahh...a year old. Her mom called and said she has colic. Dinner's on me," I lied, thinking of how Tiffany was the complete opposite of Nina in that I wouldn't ever have to stress having my daughter around Nina, because she loved her and their relationship was growing more and more every day before we broke up. They started having their own connection and spending time together outside of practice with a spa day with Samantha, Scottie, and Celine. Even teaching her how to bake and watching the excitement on Tailynn's face at the burnt brownies she attempted to make that I ate anyway, just to keep the smile on her face.

* * *

Fifteen minutes later, I made it to Samantha's place to tuck Tailynn in bed.

"Daddy, you don't look so good."

"What are you talking about?"

"I know you and Miss Nina aren't talking."

"That's nothing for you to worry about."

"I like when she's around, you seem more fun and not so mad all the time."

"What are you talking about?"

"Dad, it's me. I know you two are dating, I'm not that young, geez."

"Lil girl, if you don't go to bed."

"I hope things work out, because Miss Nina and I used to have spa days and now she doesn't come around anymore."

"I'm sorry about that, but she needs her space right now and you still get to see her at practice."

"That's true. Just remember women like jewelry."

"Who told you that?"

"Auntie Maya."

"All right, time for bed." For Tailynn to be so young, she could always sense my mood. Whenever it came to someone getting hurt or feeling sad, she would tell me to apologize and make it better. Hearing Tailynn say that she knew that something was different between Nina and I, would probably shift her relationship with Nina and I didn't want that for her. It was time for me to get things back on track.

Chapter Twenty-Four

Nina

I knew I shouldn't have gotten involved with him. Men like him only wanted one thing, and I'd served his purpose. Sitting in my office, going through the lineup for the next game, I contemplated just canceling the game altogether. I asked my assistant to check with Samantha to make sure she would drop Tailynn off for her games going forward. The less Gage and I had to be around each other, the better.

"Sorry you had to find out this way, Nina," Maya said, striding into my office and shutting the door. We were finishing up with last-minute items before we had to move off the property. I had a potential new location lined up, but it was farther out toward New Jersey, which would make it harder for some families to commute.

"It's not your fault, Maya. I should have trusted my gut and never gone out with him in the first place. You were being a friend and I appreciate you, even though I wish you didn't show my family's center on screen."

"Were your parents upset? It was a hard decision, but you know I had to do what was right."

"Yeah. Being on the other side of the media attention was something I was trying to avoid all together. I guess getting involved deeper with Gage was something that couldn't be stopped, if I'm being honest."

"If it makes you feel any better, his family has gotten bombarded with bad press ever since the story broke," Maya said taking a seat in front of my desk.

"Normally stuff like this dies down in a day or two. I'm surprised they're still talking about it almost a month later."

"His family is known for being corrupt business owners. Plus, Nationals are happening, so he's going to stay in the news until after the World Series, if they continue on this path."

"Good for him."

"How was your date the other night?" Maya inquired, taking a piece of candy out of the jar I kept for when the kids needed to come and talk to me about things that were happening in their lives.

"It was fine. He's a friend of Jackson and Genesis's. He's a billionaire in business. A little too alpha-male, cocky, and business focused for me."

"Okay." Maya shrugged nonchalantly.

"What?"

"A cocky, alpha male that has money and power. Handsome and attentive."

"What are you trying to say exactly, Maya?"

"I'm saying you have a guy that's up your ass already. Leave the rest of us single women something," Maya huffed, crossing her arms in a hissy fit.

"Maya, it was one date, and we both determined that it was best we stay friends. He's thinking of running for political office and I have more than enough drama from

Gage blowing into my life and causing drama. Second, I don't have a guy. I have my vibrator and Pornhub to satisfy me. Nothing else can compare or disappoint me if they don't show up, so I'm good."

"Okay. Well, bestie, I wanted to double check and make sure we're good. I know me delving into family business was the cause of your breakup. That wasn't my intention with exposing his father's shady dealings."

"Stop apologizing, you did your job. Was I expecting to have it plastered all over the news and social media about his family's corruption? No, but I won't dwell on the past. I take it as a lesson learned. He should have come right out and told the truth once he realized it was my family."

"Maybe he was trying to not hurt you."

"How, by lying?"

"Omitting the truth," Maya said, in air quotes.

"That's not helping us if we lose the center. Think about it from my perspective, if I would have known sooner then maybe we would have gotten a head start on the media with the news. The money he donated from the auction didn't cover us to buy the building straight out like we'd hoped. We did fix some things up from the basketball court, to the restrooms and were able to get caught up on outstanding bills and taxes for a little bit of time, and then his father had an injunction filed. The man was determined to win at any cost."

"Just say the word and I'll find an illegitimate child, or him not paying his taxes. Ohh, maybe he killed somebody and buried the bodies underneath his big ass mansion."

"You're starting to sound like Nicole. Enough about me, how is your dating life?" Standing up out of my seat I grabbed a bottle of water and my keys to head out to the field as the kids were getting dropped off Maya followed.

I attempted to quickly change the subject. All this talk of Gage was only dredging up feelings I didn't want to handle, even with a bottle of tequila. Tailynn wasn't here today because of her mom's wedding rehearsal. I waved to Celine and Kaylee as Scottie walked toward us with her hair pulled back into a high bun, showing off her latest tattoo of Celine's name on her arm that I'm assuming Talbot recently did. Celine ran up to her, grabbing her equipment bag she must have forgot.

"Ladies, how are we doing today?" she asked, taking off her shades, hugging us both, and tucking them into her pocket.

"Nothing much, I came to see how this one was doing and now I'm heading out for lunch with a friend," Maya replied, popping a piece of gum in her mouth. She pulled out her mirror and applied another coat of red lipstick.

"Someone's getting fancy for a date?"

Scottie and I giggled at Maya as she poked out her tongue in jest.

"Maya doesn't date." She felt elated by her new objectivity.

"Maya needs to stop talking about herself in the third person. Spill the beans, we've already dealt with my issues, what about you?"

"What issues do you have, NiNi?" Scottie inquired.

"Celine, grab the bat and Kaylee, you go up to pitch. I want to see how you've improved," I demanded, blowing my whistle for the girls to get in place.

"Gage is one, what else do you have an issue with?" Maya tilted her head, hand waving around as she gestured for me to respond.

"Ohh."

"Maya, I can speak for myself," I said.

Kaylee warmed up with sideways drive pitching drills. A habit she needed to work on constantly to help strengthen her pitching skills for next season.

"Are we having a girls' night tonight before we head to Talbot's event?" Scottie questioned.

"I'm not going," I responded, picking up my whistle to call time out.

"Nina, really? Talbot and Diya want you there. This is his second tattoo shop opening and all his friends are coming," Maya stated, annoyance clearly seeping into her tone.

"Please tell me you're not letting a man-"

"I'm not ready to see him yet. Send Talbot and Diya my love."

* * *

Later that evening, I found myself sitting in front of my parents' TV, eating ice cream and watching the latest celebrity news. They had all the famous stars, and New York elite, walking the red carpet and taking photos in front of Talbot's new tattoo shop. Gage came into view and he was looking as good as ever with his trimmed beard and crisp jeans and dress shirt. I noticed that he had cut his hair, and a few celebrities stood next to him posing for the cameras.

"Keep staring, but it won't make the pain go away," my dad stated plainly, coming out of the kitchen and taking a seat next to me on the couch. I lowered my head in his lap like I used to do when I was a little girl and we talked about what was upsetting me, or who he should beat up.

"Is it that obvious?"

"He looks just as miserable as you. I can promise you that."

"Why are men stupid?" I wondered out loud. He grinned, taking the ice cream out of my hand, and delving inside.

"Your mother was just like you growing up and caused me all types of hell."

"Didn't you always tell us that it was love at first sight?"

He almost choked on the ice cream from laughing at my comment.

"Baby, don't compare our relationship to what you have with him. Every relationship is different. I think you should take some time to yourself and figure out what you really want."

Agreeing with his statement, I picked up the remote off the table and changed the channel to the latest baseball playoff game.

Chapter Twenty-Five

Gage

"Are you listening to me, Gage?" Samantha commanded, nudging me in the shoulder.

I'd dozed off, thinking about the look on Nina's face when she found out about my family and their part in the fight to save the community center. The double date that Marcus and I had gone on was a complete disaster. Tiffany was straight up insane, and a groupie. The minute she found out I was her date, she did nothing but flirt and throw herself at me. If my dick didn't get hard for anyone but Nina's pussy, I probably would have taken her back to my hotel.

"Sorry, what did you say?" I asked, kissing Tailynn on her cheek as she stood in her little bridesmaid's dress, putting the finishing touches on her makeup.

Today was Samantha's wedding day, and it was a small event with only her family, Jacob's family, and a few of my family members invited. Samantha had asked me if she should uninvite my parents, but I told her that it was her day. I didn't need to speak to them, as long as they stayed out of my way.

"Daddy, you look really handsome," Li'l Bit said, taking my hand and leading me out of the room behind her mom.

I was going to walk her down the aisle, which a lot of people found strange—us included. Samantha was honestly one of my best friends, and over the years, our love had grown from a sexual relationship into best friends that loved each other for what we created. But we were not in love anymore. Jacob was a good guy, and I was happy that Samantha had found her true love. The wedding was happening in Samantha's parents' backyard. Samantha was never a traditional type of person, and I loved her for being herself and never following what the trends or society wanted her to be.

"You don't look so bad yourself, Li'l Bit," I responded, tapping her nose as she giggled.

Tailynn lined up as Jacob stood at the end of the aisle that held a long, white carpet, white chairs, and a large canopy arch. The ceremony went off without a hitch, and once the vows were said the reception moved over to the Waldorf, where Samantha saw all the stars have events at. It held close to five hundred guests, with windows on the sides that allowed a cool breeze to waft through the room and a glass roof where the sunset could be seen. Their color scheme was the same from the church with their initials S and J on the wall. For Tailynn, they ordered a candy bar for her and her friends. I was sitting with a chocolate fondue stand, a make your own candied apple, then an ice cream and yogurt bar with what seemed like a hundred flavors to choose from. Basically, it was a dentist's worst nightmare. The entree was either steak, salmon, or chicken with a variety of vegetables, such as carrots, steamed broccoli, or roasted potatoes. I stood off to the side and watched Jacob and Samantha dancing with Tailynn. She giggled and hugged his legs. It reminded me of what a wedding with Nina would have been like.

"Hi, son," my father interrupted, breaking me out of my trance.

"This isn't the time." I tried to walk off and my dad reached out to grab my arm to stop me from leaving.

"I'm sorry, you were right."

"About?"

"Everything, your mother threatened to leave me if I didn't make things right with you. She misses you and she normally doesn't get involved in any of my business dealings. Once she saw the strain between everyone, or her lack of seeing her granddaughter as much, she told me to fix what I broke or lose her forever."

"What conclusion did you come up with?"

"Son, I'm too old to try again, so I'm here waving the white flag to see if I can make things better with you and Nina."

"I don't know if it'll ever be right with her, but you can give her family back the property before the move out date."

"Will you forgive your old man? I promise I won't pull you into any more deals or pursue any more properties that cause families to lose their jobs or resources."

"I'll believe it when I see it. Coming to me now is the first step, and I know Samantha is looking over here and I don't want her to worry on her big day, so we need to wrap this up."

"Yep, and because my husband is looking too good not to rip off his clothes," Samantha teased, blowing a kiss to Jacob.

I shook hands with my father and watched as he walked over to sit next to my mother and brother. Samantha circled her arm in mine as the music started and everyone stood up.

"Don't let love pass you over because of a mistake," Samantha said, grinning and waving at everyone taking pictures and smiling.

"Today is about you."

"I know, and I appreciate you for everything you've done for me, Gage, and your happiness means a lot to me, as well. You may not know this, but Tailynn tells me you haven't been yourself lately, and I know it's because of Nina."

Reaching the dance floor, I kissed her on both of her cheeks and whispered low in her ear, tightening my grip as we danced. Jacob walked up to steal his wife away for a dance after the song ended, and while we've become friends over the years, I still needed to let him know that Samantha had me in her corner if she ever needed anything. Any guy that hurt her would answer to me.

"Take care of her," I said reaching out to shake hands with Jacob and returning to the table in the front row with her family.

Chapter Twenty-Six

Nina

It was a lively game, with press sitting near the cages taking photos, and local reporters lining up like this was the World Series. I expected it was because of Tailynn being shown across multiple television screens as the daughter of Gage Young. I knew that he tried his best to keep her out of the limelight, but more than likely, it was from all the controversy that his family was embroiled in with the media over uprooting local businesses and putting families out on the streets.

"Let's go, April, you got this!" I encouraged, clapping and motioning for the crowd to help cheer her on. She had the same speed and talent as Tailynn, but she'd taken more time to practice and focus on improving her skills at catching and hitting the ball to get more playing time. Her speed was a major factor in giving her the start. I heard loud screams and cheers as Tailynn slid to first base. Her excitement brought me back to my time playing professionally.

***

2015 Women's Softball World Championships

The glare of the lights was jarring as I stepped up to the plate. This was my final chance before retiring—something I hadn't discussed with my family. The announcer said my name, and my jersey flashed across the screen as I pulled a cool breath in and pushed it out, letting the nerves release. We were going up against a long-standing rival— Japan.

Wiping the sweat from across my brow, I craned my neck, stretching my left, then right arm. Gripping the handle of the bat, I zoned in on the pitcher narrowing her eyes with a small smirk dancing across her lips.

She circled the ball in her hands, once, twice, raised her leg, turning to the side, stepping into the plate throwing the ball at a high speed. My heart was beating out of my chest. I had to prepare to fulfill my life-long dream, or end my career without a ring.

"Go, Nina! Go!" I heard my mother scream as my eyes bulged and the ball shot through the sky. I dropped the bat and took off running as my team members screamed at me to run. I charged around the field, running from one base to the other as the ball went past the outfield. Everyone was up on their feet, cheering me on. It was like a movie of my life playing out on the big screen, it was so surreal.

When I finally made it back to home base, I released a hard breath and hugged my sister, who had ran out onto the field.

As the sign changed to World Champions, I let the tears I was holding fall.

***

"Nina! Nina, did you see me?" April ran over and hugged me around the waist.

We high-fived and I told her, "Great job!"

Turning to watch her walk back over to the bench, I noticed the last person I expected to see today standing at the gate, wearing a hat and dark black shades. He stood off to the side; I assumed to not cause a disruption for the girls, since today was all about them. Ignoring the growing pain that I felt for not being able to touch him or feel him near, I turned back around to continue coaching the game, since we stood 3-4 currently.

***

It was our normal Sunday dinner. Romi was sitting next to me, breastfeeding her new baby as Nicholas talked with our father.

"Granny, how was church today?" Nicole inquired, passing the bowl of mac and cheese to her. Nicole wore faux locks in her hair and came over after finishing her shift at the local sex shop, where she worked part-time during the week while she figured out her goals. This was yet another persona she was trying out to keep from really growing up and being a responsible adult.

"Church was good, baby. It would have been better if you showed up like you promised?"

"Sorry, work was crazy busy today."

"Nicole you don't work," Nicholas said.

Romi and I snickered at my brother putting her on blast.

"Mind your own business, Nicholas," Nicole spat.

"Shade," Grandfather joked, high fiving me.

"Grandpa!" Nicole shouted in frustration at being the brunt of our family jokes.

"Don't yell at my husband because you're being sneaky and underhanded about the Lord," Granny said, taking a delicate sip of her lemonade.

"I wasn't being sneaky. Besides, the Lord is with me at all times. He understands the work I do helps people."

"What the hell is a rump shop?" Granddaddy leaned forward, turning his hearing aid up as Romi burst out laughing.

"A sex shop," I snitched, telling all her business.

Granny really couldn't talk about anybody because she gambles.

"Nicole, really, out of all of my kids, I expected a little more respect for our family from you. What do you think everyone in the church will think when word gets out about you working in a sex shop?" Mother questioned disappointedly. She shook her head, stood up and walked to the kitchen.

"Honey, leave her alone. She's still finding herself, at her age I was doing a lot worse than her, from smoking, drinking..." Granny described before Nicholas cut her off.

"Grandma, please keep that kind of thing to yourself," Nicholas insisted, shaking his head.

"Boy, I'm grown. How do you think your momma got here?" Granny pointed out, with our grandfather.

"All right, time for me to go," I said, before standing up, grabbed my purse and keys, and headed toward the front door. I opened it right when a knock was heard.

"Why are you here?"

Chapter Twenty-Seven

Nina

"I wanted to apologize to your family and you," Tobias Young stated as I held the door of my family's home open.

A part of me wanted to slam the door in his face after all the bullshit he'd caused. The other part knew that this was Tailynn's grandfather, and I loved that little girl with all my heart. I stood to the side, so he could come in.

"Well, speak of the devil and he shall appear," Granny snickered, then stood up and walked off. Mom went to follow behind her.

"I won't keep you long, Nina."

"If you're here about your son, then you can rest assured we aren't seeing each other anymore."

"I know, and that's why I came to apologize. Gage and I have a strained relationship, and it became even more strained with the situation of your family's business."

"You mean the business you tried to demolish?" Grandfather questioned. Mr. Young nodded his head in agreement.

"Let's give them some privacy, everyone," my father said, and everyone walked away, leaving us alone.

"Would you like to have a seat?"

"Thank you. I won't keep you long, Nina. As you can tell, apologizing isn't something I'm used to doing." Tobias chuckled. Not getting a reaction out of me, he cleared his throat and continued, "I want to give you back the deed to your family's property free and clear."

"What's the catch?"

"No catch. We—or, I—shouldn't have tried to move in on your property. I love my granddaughter, and it may seem like I only think about money, but that little girl holds my heart in the palm of her hand. Honestly, seeing my family broken was something I couldn't handle any longer, especially knowing I was the cause of the rift. Again, I was wrong and I apologize for causing any harm to your family. Hard thing to swallow, not seeing my family because I hurt someone they loved," Tobias said, pulling out the deed to the property.

"I don't want you hating my son, Nina; it was me that caused all this confusion. My son and I have disagreed on my business dealings with rental properties and it has caused fights and we've suffered broken trust between us for years now. I wanted you to know that I donated to your center and plan on in the future to look deeper before buying up property and kicking people out."

"How do I know he didn't put you up to coming here and lying?"

"Currently he's not speaking to me, and he's refused to let my wife or I see our grandchild."

He passed the envelope over to me, and I opened it and peered at the paperwork it contained. It showed my name as the owner.

"Please call my cell, or even better come to his game tomorrow night as his guest," Tobias suggested.

"Does he know you're here?"

Tobias nodded and walked back toward the door.

I followed behind him, opening the door so he could leave.

"Please think about coming. It's Nationals which determines the teams for the World Series."

"Thank you for apologizing, but I can't promise that I'll show up tomorrow. Tell Gage I said good luck," I answered and shut the door, walking back to the couch to look over the paperwork for the building.

The blogs had him only going to the stadium and home. No late night parties or dates, all of the women seemed to be cut off. Even Talbot called me one day talking about how miserable Gage was without me. I'm conflicted over wanting to be with him at the same time not giving in too fast. I guessed I held him to a higher standard when it came to my heart and knowing he could easily hurt me in a split second intentionally or not was a wakeup call for me. Gage Young wasn't perfect, but then again neither was I.

One week ago

"Talbot, I don't want to hear any excuses. You of course will take up for your friend if that will get him up off your couch. Diya told me he's been hanging out more at the tattoo shop or your place to avoid being home alone."

"Nina, you should see him. I've known Gage for a long time and usually he's the one dumping the women and moving on fast. Lately he hasn't shaved, almost missed a practice before the big game, Marcus was telling me he was even ignoring Samantha's calls."

"He made his bed, so now he needs to deal with the consequences."

"Does that extend to you both being miserable because you're too stubborn to forgive and stop comparing him to your past boyfriends?" Talbot inquired.

He was right, but I was stubborn. I can admit I still carried old wounds, from one boyfriend cheating, and another one wanting to get with me because of the fame that came with my career. Even Maya found old posts of Gage in the blogs with different women on his arm every other day. Some of them were even during our courtship. My fear of giving in and thinking he wasn't ready was the big fear. Most often dating in the public eye brought on more drama because they wanted to know every detail of our lives. With me coaching locally I didn't need to deal with having people stalk every move I made, or having women try and fight me because I was dating a famous athlete.

"Come to the game, it's the Nationals and he could use all of our support, NiNi. I know you're upset with him, but I know deep down you still love him," Diya demanded, on the other line. Oh, hell. They had me on a three-way call.

"I don't think that's good idea. We need a clean break."

"If you believe that, NiNi, you wouldn't have stayed on this call talking about him for so long," Diya stated plainly.

The entire situation was weird because we have the same friends and I didn't want to be near him if they brought him around.

"How was your grand opening of your second bike shop, Talbot?"

"Nice change of subject. It was fine, everyone showed

up and we tattooed a few people. It was mostly about the new team that would be running the shop and letting them shine."

"Genesis and Scottie showed up, Nicole was even there for a bit," Diya responded.

"My sister didn't tell me she went."

"Yep, and she was dressed for the occasion in her biker gear and wanting to get a tattoo and work in the shop. I had her sit to get drawn and pick out a design. Soon as I put the stencil up to her arm, she jumped like she'd been shot. I laughed so hard," Talbot said, giving me all the gossip about my sister.

"Did Maya come and cover the event for her show? I saw some of the footage with you guys walking the red carpet on one of the entertainment news channels."

"She did, and talked with Gage about everything. He's forgiven her, so maybe it's time you do the same thing with him," Diya said quietly.

"Look at the time, I have an early day tomorrow. Let's catch up over lunch later in the week," I insisted.

"You can't run from love forever, NiNi," Diya said as we all said our goodbyes.

Chapter Twenty-Eight

Gage

t Nationals

The stadium was sold out, people even tried hitting me up on social media to get tickets. I stood in the locker room, nervous that she wouldn't show. I missed seeing her face, hearing her voice, even if she was upset. Falling for her wasn't ever in the plan.

Tailynn told me that she called and begged Nina to show up today, and I hated that she was caught up in the middle of the drama. This was supposed to be the best time in our lives as we were possibly heading into another World Series run.

"All right, fellas, it's go time!" Coach yelled.

I tightened up my glove and checked my helmet and gear. Marcus was in the corner with his eyes closed, meditating like always. I had all our friends and family here in the box helping me with my surprise, if things worked out in my favor that is.

Nicole was supposed to text me if her sister agreed to come and time was running out. The second I stepped onto the field, all other thoughts went out the window.

Checking my phone one last time, it buzzed with a message from Nicole.

Nicole: *The bird is home.*

Me: *?*

Nicole: *The chicken has come to roost.*

Me: *What?*

Nicole: *Damn, man, pull your head out of your ass... it's a metaphor. Nina is here.*

Me: *My bad, thanks.*

I turned my phone off and followed the rest of the team out into the corridor.

The announcer called us up to the plate and we all waved as the crowd went wild. The stadium was packed as both sides, Raptors and Los Angeles Devils, shook hands to signal good sportsmanship.

As the coin was tossed, we won first bat. The announcer came on right as my plan was going into play.

"Ladies and gentlemen, the New York Raptors are first up, and hometown starter, Gage Young, is up to catch. Before we begin, we need to direct everyone's attention to the Jumbotron," the announcer said as I walked out onto the field.

Pictures of Nina and me were displayed up on the screen. The crowd erupted, and flashing lights went off as I made it out onto the field. Nina was being escorted out to me. I bent down on one knee right as the screen read, *"Will you marry me, babydoll?"*

Her family screamed and jumped for joy. Nina ran toward me, and I almost fell as we collided. She kissed all over my face as I tried to get the words out. "Baby... will you...?"

"Yes. Yes..."

"Babydoll, I've screwed up a lot of things in my life, so let me do this one right. Nina Mitchell, I'm a man of few words, as you know. I've made some mistakes, but I will work hard for the rest of my life if you'll have me. Will you do me the honor of being my wife?"

She nodded as tears fell down her cheeks and I placed the five-carat emerald cut ring on her finger and she kissed me over and over again.

"Yes, Gage, I'll marry you."

Hearing her calling me Gage instead of her normal sassy "Mr. Young," made my heart sing. I yanked her close to my chest, kissing her long and hard.

The cheers and joy around us continued as I stood and kissed her once again. I escorted her off the field, kissing her ring finger.

Then, it was time to go to work; I had a game to win for my fiancée.

***

Once the game was over, I knew the only place I wanted to be was around Nina and Li'l Bit. Instead of celebrating with the team, I drove to her family's home with Tailynn. As soon as the car stopped, I pulled the key out of the ignition, and Tailynn jumped out of the car. I called her name to get her to stop rushing.

"Li'l Bit, slow down, you know better."

"Sorry, Daddy, I forgot."

I always fussed at Tailynn for attempting to run off. It was my job to open all doors for the women in my life and be her protector. Kissing Nina on the cheek, I opened the door and walked around to the passenger side and grabbed her trophy that she had brought from home to show Nina's family.

Tailynn ran off toward the front door, not waiting for us. I helped Nina out of the car, pushed her up against the car and made up for lost time by kissing her deep and long. Not seeing her every day and night had been painful. No one could replace her sassy, stubborn, sexy attitude.

"You do know we have people waiting on us?" Nina asked, nudging my hand from running across her soft skin in the little dress she wore.

"Let's leave Li'l Bit here and go celebrate together alone," I said, groaning, as I pulled her in close by the hip against my straining erection, which was growing by the minute.

She snickered under her breath. Nina was toying with me. She pushed me back and took my hand, walking toward her parents' home. Tailynn ran inside and slammed the door in her haste to get inside.

Nina turned the knob and walked inside as I followed behind her as loud laughs were heard echoing throughout the room.

"Ohh, he's cute. Are you related to that dancer boy on that movie? Manny, Melvin." Her grandmother snapped her fingers trying to think of what I could only assume was that *Magic Mike* lead actor, Channing Tatum. Often, I would get the whole you're either the guy from *Sons of Anarchy* or Channing Tatum because of my beard.

"Do you mean *Magic Mike*, Grandma?" Nicole inquired, chuckling at her grandmother staring at me lustfully.

"Grandma, you have a husband and he's sitting right there," Nina said leading me to the couch. This was where everyone was cackling as her husband regarded her in amusement, knowing she was a spitfire. I could see Nina and myself acting the same way once we reached their ages.

"And I could have yours too if you don't act right," her grandmother, Doretha, stated.

I howled at her response, bending over holding my stomach. I get hit on a lot, but never by a woman in her seventies; this was a whole new ballgame for me.

Nina's brow pulled into an affronted frown. "Gage, stop laughing. All you're doing is egging her on. Ma, what did you cook?" Nina pecked my lips and I wasn't satisfied. I gripped the back of her head, and reclaimed her lips and I crushed her to my chest. My tongue traced the soft fullness of her lips, and explored the recesses of her mouth.

Hearing someone clear their throat, she pulled back hastily. "You're still my little girl, and making out with your boyfriend in my house won't happen," her father argued, pointing between the both of us.

"Sorry, Daddy."

"You're fine, baby," her father and I both replied at the same time. She buried her face in my neck in embarrassment. I wrapped an arm around her waist and mouthed sorry to him and the entire room laughed at her expense.

"Don't worry, Pops, you still have one innocent daughter," Nicole said, winking her left eye at her sister behind her father's back.

"Let me move away from you, because that lie will cause lightning to strike any minute," Doretha responded. The entire evening, we listened to stories about Nina growing up, along with her siblings. The laughs never stopped.

Chapter Twenty-Nine

Gage

Letting Tailynn spend the night with Nicole was a big step for me. Since her mom was away on her honeymoon, and my parents had decided to go on a cruise, I'd let Tailynn talk me into letting her have a sleepover with Nicole. Nina was more worried than I was; it was funny how they bickered so much—and yet, if anyone else tried to talk about them, they'd find themselves in a huge fight.

After our dinner at her family's home, I wanted to be alone with my future wife. She was everything to me, and I wouldn't let anything hinder our relationship. Pushing my father to end his bid on her family's center hadn't been an easy task, but I finally decided to let the stress go and focus on what I could control for my future. I spoke with Genesis who'd agreed to back me up. I sold my share in my family's company to him, and they helped invest in opening up more centers in other at-risk neighborhoods to start afterschool programs and more softball teams for kids of all ages.

We had the penthouse to ourselves for the weekend,

and I planned to be in bed for the duration, naked. I grazed her earlobe with a quick kiss, needing to show her that I meant every word of my proposal. She buried her face against my throat, and my hands explored the hollows of her back.

A deep feeling of peace entered my being. Our lives were becoming one and Tailynn would one day have brothers and sisters. Nina was going to be my wife.

She drew in a shallow breath.

"Are you sure about this Gage?" Nina asked, letting a little doubt creep in as she held her breath.

"Babydoll, you can't get rid of me that easily," I said, my mouth twisting into a smirk.

Her stare heated my skin. I craved her touch. As our lips converged, the slow penetration of her tongue pushed to gain entry. Memories of our first night together flooded back. I picked her up, and she wrapped her legs around me. I pushed her up against the wall in my bedroom. She helped loosen my belt, and I ripped off the flimsy thong she was wearing as her wetness seeped out.

My strokes moved even faster against her. I leaned my forehead against hers and smacked a hand against the wall, as her warm pussy held a tight grip around my shaft. Our appetite for each other was ravenous. Her pussy squeezed and as I pounded, I met her thrust for thrust, while she clawed at my back.

"Shh... baby," I growled as the intense pressure of her tight core made me strain to get out the few words that I could. She had me speechless.

"You're at my spot, baby, ugh... God!" she moaned, burying her face in my neck.

I watched the pleasure play across her face as I continued to slam between her wet folds.

* * *

I ran a hand across her thick thigh as we sat in bed, eating a host of junk food. She had a craving for ice cream, pizza, and cookies. I would never deny her anything, so I heated up some leftover food, and we just hung out and talked about everything we missed out on during the time we were apart.

"I went out on a date!" Nina suddenly blurted out.

"I know. I had seen a photo of you with someone, but it was too blurry to make out. Who was it?" I questioned.

"Scottie and Genesis's friend, Ethan."

"Ethan West?"

"You know him?" She looked up into my eyes. I tried to not have an annoyed look cross my face, even though I was pissed off on the inside. I learned to suppress my attitude and not scare her off again.

"He's an old associate of my family. We've had issues in the past from him dating Samantha while we were broken up."

"Time to change the subject, because I can tell you're turning red in the face. But I just wanted you to know that nothing happened, in the interest of full disclosure. Now, how is everything with your family?" Nina pushed a spoonful of ice cream over to me. It was her favorite, chocolate chip ice cream. The conversation about my family was something I'm glad she waited to bring up until after we finished having sex. Last thing I needed was to think about anything that would cause my orgasm to diminish.

"We're in a good place now. Things were rocky for a while after the scandal came out. My father only sees dollar signs. Don't get me wrong, he loves his family, just that for a long time money was his motivation in life."

"Did he tell you about coming to my parents' house?" Nina inquired.

"Yeah, because I stopped going over to the house and kept Tailynn away after the entire blow up."

She nodded in understanding of keeping Tailynn away from my family. Nina knew how much I valued family above all else. "You would really not speak to your parents over what happened with us?"

Taking the ice cream out of her hand and placing it on the nightstand, I pulled her down to lay on her back. I squeezed between her legs. The only thing keeping my dick from sliding back in was the pair of boxers I wore, and the thin sheet that was covering her naked body.

"Baby, you are the woman I love, and if someone hurts you or my daughter, I make sure to hurt back even worse. Nothing comes before you or Tailynn in my life," I said firmly, as I tenderly glided a hand across her cheek. She eased a leg around my waist.

"I have to admit; before getting to know the real you, I thought this cocky attitude of yours was a complete turn-off."

"What made you change your mind about me?"

"Tailynn," she answered.

"Really?"

"Yep. Seeing how you treat your daughter and the love she has for you through her eyes opened my heart to giving you another chance. What made you get the tattoo?" She reached up and traced the design.

"I wanted to keep you close to me."

"What if I never would have forgiven you?"

"That's a thought I'd never allow to take up real estate in my mind."

"There's the cocky guy I know."

"I'm glad you gave us another chance."

"Me, too," Nina said softly, smiling as her hand gripped my hard dick.

Being close to her—or even just looking at her—caused all my senses to leave. The next day my mother called about coming over for dinner with Tailynn, and Nina said I should, and to stop being stubborn. Once Li'l Bit started fussing about not seeing her grandmother as much as she used to, I had to agree. I still held a little bitterness about things, but in time, I think the relation-ship between my father and I could grow into a better space. The final game was approaching for the World Series and next to making Nina my wife, nothing else really mattered. Once we finished off the season, I could have more time to be a husband and get things situated with slowing down my career and focusing on Nina and Tailynn. A few days later, I was at dinner with my parents and Tailynn was showing her Uncle Gordon the latest nail polish color she had picked out during a spa day with Nina. This was the first time in a while I'd come over after the situation with trying to push her family out of business.

"Gage, are you ready for the big day?" my mom asked, taking a bite of her asparagus.

Picking up my napkin I politely wiped the rim of my mouth. "Of course, Mom. The team is looking good going into the last game, so no doubt we will pull it off, and now that I got my girl back with me, everything is lining up right."

"Bro, I bet a lot of money on you guys. I'm expecting a

nice return on my investment. Don't mess this up," Gordon, my younger brother, taunted.

"Gordon, we don't gamble in this family," Mother said, narrowing her eyes in anger.

"Tailynn, how is school going, baby?" Father quickly steered the conversation back to safer ground.

"Fine, my teacher is having a bring your parents to work day and I asked Daddy if I could have Nina come and talk this year instead of him."

"That's nice of her." Mother smiled, taking a sip of water.

"My wife's the best," I announced and everyone almost choked on their meal.

Chapter Thirty

Nina

One week later...

We were sitting in the box seats for the final game of the World Series. Everyone was there: Diya, Samantha, Scottie, Tailynn, Gage's parents, and all my family and friends. In two weeks, I would be Mrs. Gage Young, and I was still in disbelief that the same guy whom I'd bumped into twice, with the same cocky attitude, was about to become my husband. He'd proposed that Samantha should put the finishing touches on our wedding day, and I had Maya and Nicole already making plans.

"Nina, when are you two going on your honeymoon?" Diya asked, passing me a drink.

I didn't have the heart to tell her that I thought I might be pregnant, so I took the drink politely and placed it next to me on the chair. Gage and I weren't really using protection anymore, and I knew that if I got pregnant, he'd be a great father just from seeing him with Tailynn, and the way he treated Genesis's kids, along with his nieces and nephews.

"Not long after the wedding. We both have a lot of work to get caught up on, now that the season is over and we can really enjoy being a family. Scottie, how did you deal with being a stepmother in the beginning?"

"It was oddly fine, and Celine's a good kid which made it even better. The challenges aren't an end all, be all, because of dating a guy with a kid. You have to look at it as you both growing together and making it your family and establishing your rules. Having an open and honest relationship with the child separate from the guy I believe helps make the adult relationship stronger."

"I love Tailynn and she definitely makes me a better person," I answered.

"You remember that date with Ethan West?" Scottie asked with a gleam in her eyes.

"What about it?" I inquired.

Scottie passed me her phone. On the screen was a picture of Ethan on a double date with her and Genesis, along with a business friend of theirs—another cocky, arrogant asshole of a billionaire. His wealth was in banking. Our chemistry was more of friendship than anything sexual. I did have someone in mind for him, but getting her to go on a blind date would be a little bit of a tough situation. She was on a celibacy kick at the moment, and I knew just from talking to him on our little date that he wouldn't last long without sex. He probably stayed in a different woman's bed every other night.

"I think he would be perfect for Maya." Scottie mischievously winked; I could see the matchmaking wheels turning overtime in her mind.

"That's a disaster waiting to happen," I chuckled giving her phone back to her before taking a sip of the water.

"Wait and see me work my magic," Scottie sternly stated, taking a sip of her drink.

"I'm pregnant," I whispered.

"Ahhhh! This calls for a drink. Well not for you, but me," Scottie teased.

Now that she was done with breastfeeding she was making up for lost time. Feeling like an official part of the clique, I realized this was my group of friends that I could talk about anything with and who would help me understand the world we lived in with the men in our lives.

The next day I arrived at the gym to meet up with Gage to work out. He gave me a good workout last night, and early this morning. Before meeting up with me at the gym, he had an early morning interview with a local newspaper about the new charity organization he was breaking ground on that would benefit local businesses in the city.

"Babydoll, you miss me?" Gage joked, approaching me from behind, grabbing me around the waist, and kissing the back of my neck.

"I did. How was the interview?"

He moved around to my front, pecking me on the forehead. I followed him as we headed to a private area of the gym, and he tapped the workout bench for me to sit on as he leaned back to lift weights.

"The interview was good. A ton of press showed up, and of course, nonstop photographers, wanting the inside scoop on our upcoming wedding. I kept the details out of the press so we wouldn't have any issues once we said 'I do'," Gage reassured me.

"Thank you, what about Maya and her show?'

"What about it?"

"She wants to make amends and apologize for dragging you through the mud," I teased, kissing his lips and standing up to head to the other side of the gym and grab the smaller weights. I remembered our second time bumping into each other, when we were at the gym. Visions of him thinking he was the sports version of Eminem doing his own version of Cardi B's song "Press," flashed through my mind.

"I'll pass."

"Gage, don't be an asshole. Yes, she made a mistake, but it all started with your family. I don't want to argue about this," I grunted as I counted to twenty in my head while I lifted the dumbbells.

"What do I get if I forgive her?" Gage goaded me, walking up behind me and placing a hand against the wall. He pushed my chest gently up against the mirror.

Giggling at his so-called "manipulation," I went along with him to see how far he'd go. I pushed my ass against his groin, and he grumbled under his breath. I turned around and squatted in front of him. His eyebrows furrowed in surprise.

"What would you like?"

"You."

"You already have me," I pursued him, sliding my hand into his basketball shorts.

A hitch in his breath caused his head to fall back.

"Forever," he spoke in a low whisper.

"Forever, Mr. Young," I moaned. He looked around the room and spotted the locker room and strode over and opened the door, quickly checking if anyone was inside. After locking the door, I pushed him against the wall and dropped to my knees pulling out his dick. I stroked him slowly up to the tip and he moaned lowly as I took his dick into my mouth until it hit the back of my throat. Forever sounded pretty fucking good to me.

Chapter Thirty-One

Nina

Gage hadn't spared any expense after I said yes to his marriage proposal. I wasn't that into huge weddings, but with Nicole and Maya in my ear, along with Romi, who was feeling the tug of her and my brother one day walking down the aisle, I insisted that they help plan everything. The rehearsal dinner was wonderful, and everyone showed up. A lot of our community center kids were invited. The pastor was a friend of the family who couldn't wait to perform the ceremony because of the celebrity guests who were attending. One thing I did demand was to keep our wedding details out of the press, and Gage made sure to let his publicist and manager know that any paparazzi who came near us should be escorted out by the police.

I was pleasantly surprised that Scottie, Diya, and Samantha had all agreed to be bridesmaids. We'd grown closer over these past few months, and I considered them to be my sister-circle. Tailynn was my flower girl and took the job very seriously. She'd set times to go visit flower shops with her mom to test out the best arrangements. She wanted the colors to all blend well with our dresses.

Honestly, I felt beyond blessed with all the support.

We were currently standing in the bride's room of the church, getting our last-minute makeup touches. Gage had flown in a French designer from Paris to create the perfect gown that was shown at Paris Fashion Week—a romantic, vintage-inspired lace trumpet gown with a V-neck that plunged at the back for a spine-tingling finish. Maya had almost lost her mind when I had the fitting. All of the bridal party wore light-blue, sleeveless, floor-length gowns that buttoned on the side, with Gage's player number sewn in small numerals beside the buttons.

"Nina, do you need anything before I go out to check on everyone?" Mom asked affectionately, inspecting my makeup.

My "something new" was my dress; my "something borrowed" was his game winning ball he caught for the World Series, "something old" was a pendent my grandmother gave to me. My "something blue," which I hadn't told anyone other than Scottie, was that I was pregnant. Two days ago, feeling nauseous and tired, I decided to take a pregnancy test. The two blue lines confirmed that I was pregnant. Next week, I'd have an official appointment with a doctor.

"Mommy, when do we start?" Tailynn asked Samantha as she tried to finish putting her hair up in a bun.

I smiled, looking over at them. Samantha and Jacob were the prime example of a blended family, and how to make things work as a partnership. Gage was very protective of his daughter, and somehow, he'd been able to make it work with Jacob and show Tailynn that Jacob was a bonus person in her life. Now, I was a bonus person too. Our bond had started even before I knew she was the daughter of a famous athlete.

"In a few minutes, Tai. It's Nina's day, so we have to wait on her before we start," Samantha said cheerfully, kissing the top of her daughter's head.

There was a knock on the door, and Diya and Scottie walked inside with the pastor. "You look so beautiful, NiNi!" Scottie stated excitedly, hugging Samantha, Nicole, and my mom.

"Thanks, Scottie. How is everything out there? Is Gage ready?"

She grinned amusedly. "That man is ready to steal you away. I had Genesis and Talbot keep him company."

"This reminds me so much of you and Genesis, and how you two started; I never imagined complete opposites falling in love and getting married," Diya reminded us, and we all nodded in agreement, and laughed at Scottie, who was rolling her eyes as she remembered their courtship that started on a train ride.

"Ladies, we have about ten minutes to all get lined up," Maya said. "NiNi, you should see the decorations; everything is so nice and luxurious."

"Are the men ready?" I asked, standing, and grabbing my bouquet of white roses from Scottie.

"Yep—and if we keep Gage waiting any longer, he's going to 'come in here and drag you out to the justice of the peace,' and I quote," Scottie said in her best Gage impression, making air quotes with her fingers.

I giggled at her and gazed at all my friends and family, thinking of the next journey I would explore. My softball team was finally getting the recognition they deserved, and Tailynn was more focused and playing better after

Gage had started helping with her training. Becoming a mom would bring things full-circle.

"I'm ready to become Mrs. Gage Young," I said, delighted, and pulled the veil over my face.

The church music started as we all piled out of the room. My father came over and encircled his arm with mine, kissing me on the cheek. I watched as the doors opened, and I was struck in amazement at the display they'd set up. The room was filled with gold trim on the benches, an arch with cream roses aligned on each side, and a large sign on the side wall that Tailynn had created with Gage's and my name.

Gage stood on the top stoop, then walked down to meet me as my father let my hand go and shook hands with Gage. Gage grasped my hand, pulling it toward his lips. This man left me breathless. He wore a black Marc Jacobs tuxedo with gold cufflinks. He leaned over, caressing my cheek and whispered lovingly in my ear, "You look beautiful, babydoll." He started to pull me in close for a kiss.

"Uh, we normally save that for the end of the cere-mony, Mr. Young," the pastor said amusedly, motioning for us to face him as our guests chuckled. "Do you, Gage Young, take Nina Mitchell to be your lawfully wedded wife?"

"Ten times over, yes," Gage responded as a smile lit up his face.

"Do you, Nina Mitchell, take Gage Young to be your lawfully wedded husband to have and to hold, in sickness and in health, 'til death do you part?" the pastor questioned.

My head was spinning; I could hardly think straight.

"I do!" I said quickly, and no sooner than the words

were out of my mouth then Gage pulled me into his embrace, tilting me to the side, and kissing me long and deep. The pastor tried clearing his throat to get Gage to stop, but it never happened as everyone cheered him on.

***

Twenty minutes after saying "I do," we were kissing like two teenagers again on our first date. He pulled me close. For a moment, I pondered whether he could tell that I was a little flustered over our lip-biting kiss that had left me feeling more than a little aroused. Gage cradled me in his arms and jumped the broom at the end as the photographer took shots of us standing in front of our archway. The practice was an old traditional African symbol of two lives becoming one. Then we walked out to our limo and jumped into the car, heading to his family's estate for our reception.

His gaze wandered slowly down my body. Every nerve in my body seemed to stir with emotion. "You're sitting too far away, babydoll," Gage said, pressing me close to the warmth of his body. His touch moved down my arm to my hand.

"Mr. Young, you have to wait until after the reception before you can get any. I promise that after this, I got you, baby." I let my body sag against his as he kissed the nape of my neck.

"Did I mention how fucking sexy you look in this dress?" Gage asked, running a hand across my thigh. I felt a nervous tickle in my throat that he would find out my secret.

"I love you, and can't wait to go on our honeymoon to Fiji," I replied changing the subject.

"How long is this going to take?" he asked with a hungry look in his eyes.

I laughed low under my breath at his obvious attempt to get me alone for sex. I could tell how our honeymoon would shape up with us staying inside for the entire trip.

We arrived through the gates of his childhood home as more limos and cars lined up, and guests walked toward the backyard. I was from a family who liked to party intimately, so being stuck in some high-priced hotel had been out of the question. My parents brought some of my favorite foods, along with Gage's, which combined our styles, which ranged from down home comfort food like steak, potatoes, and artichokes, all the way to caviar, lobster, and expensive wine.

Security came around, directing traffic, and opened our door. Gage stepped out, shaking hands with his personal bodyguard with whom I'd become super close with and considered a friend. He would be the perfect person to calm Maya down.

How are you?" I asked as he grinned at us both.

"Happy to see bossman less stressed now that you're in his life again."

"Was he that bad during our breakup?" I wondered.

"Allow me to put it like this, the man wouldn't even leave the house unless it had something to do with Tailynn."

"That's enough telling all my secrets, man," Gage joked, patting him on the back.

Gage extended his hand toward me. He stared into my eyes, drawing me in close, cupping my cheek, nipping at my top lip before sweeping me into a knee-buckling kiss.

We followed the music to the backyard, where

another "field of dreams" was set up with two large tents and a dance floor. Guests mixed and mingled as Gage and I hugged and kissed our family and friends. I wasn't one for the traditional couple introduction, so we just walked over and sat at the head of the table.

"How are you feeling about the whole world knowing about us?" Gage inquired kissing the side of my cheek.

"Surprisingly okay, still shocked that I actually got married."

"This is the first of many surprises, as our lives move in tandem, babydoll. Since you've been in my life, you've taught me how to love, be patient, and compromise. Every day for the rest of our lives, I want to show you how much you mean to me."

"When you talk like that, Gage, it shows me that you're in it for the long haul and ready to have the stability that comes along with being married. I didn't trust you before, but I noticed your growth over these past few months, and I'm grateful that you fought for us when I gave up," I replied, kissing him on the lips as the music started playing, and the announcer lined up the maid of honor and the best man for toasts.

Everyone enjoyed themselves, and laughed, and loved like a big, blended family. Gage left me to go over and dance with my grandmother, cutting in between my grandfather. She giggled at his charm. He could get that reaction from anyone.

* * *

Gage spared no expense as we went to Fiji again, since we loved it so much the first time around. I felt his large body hover over mine as he stared into my eyes. I smiled reaching out to touch his cheek.

"What are you thinking about?"

I glanced around the room at the white silk curtains draped around us, as the full moon shone off to the side. This was the first night of our honeymoon after flying in on a private jet. As soon as the reception was over, we left and promised Tailynn we'd bring her back a gift. Now lying under my husband, a man that caused me so much grief and annoyance in the beginning, I couldn't feel more complete.

"Aghhh! Gage," I moaned out as he slowly thrust inside me, keeping a steady pace. Biting his bottom lip, I gripped both sides of him bringing him closer. I wanted to be drowned in his love. He was everything that I needed and more.

"I love you so much, babydoll," Gage whispered, kissing across my shoulder, snuggling in between my neck and cheek.

Our trip lasted for over two weeks with shopping, dinner, sightseeing, and snorkeling in the ocean.

"Gage, if you drop me, I'm kicking your ass!"

We had a boat that took us out to a sacred area with a series of caves that held a meaning of lasting love if you came with your partner. You're only supposed to look, but of course with Gage being himself, he decided to jump in and then bring me down with him to make sure our love is forever.

"You look beautiful like this, no makeup, just us. Take off your top."

"I'm not taking my top off." He tried to reach over and untie my top but I smacked his hand away. I snickered at his poked out lip.

"Why not, baby? I want to leave our mark in here and have you screaming my name."

"We aren't here alone," I muttered as he tried to nudge me into a corner away from prying eyes.

I giggled at his mischief.

"They won't see. I'll ask them to turn around. We can say years from now that we did something spontaneous." He gripped both my legs wrapping them around his waist. I gripped his shoulders.

"Gage!"

"Shush...shush, baby. I got you."

"I cannot believe I let you talk me into this." He smirked, removing one breast out of my yellow bikini top.

Next thing I knew, there we were in the middle of a cave, having sex.

"Shit! Hold...on...tight."

"Mhmmm...fuck...Oh God!"

The next few days consisted of breakfast in bed, sex, lunch on the beach, sex on the beach, and then dinner with oral pleasure because he'd drained me until I could barely move. He complained that he was making up for lost time during our separation. I didn't care, but the sexy time was off-limits when we got back home. That man wore me out. We kept up with Gage's tradition and Face-Timed with Tailynn almost every night to check up on her.

Chapter Thirty-Two

Gage & Nina

Three weeks later...
Gage

Ever since we got back from our honeymoon in Fiji, Nina had been distant and aloof, like she had a lot on her mind. Normally, she would have scheduled all the games and practices; work at the center had always been her top priority, but lately, she was pawning it off on her brother and sister. Her assistant had taken on more responsibility, and I didn't think anything of it at first. Other than that, our lives hadn't changed too much since Nina had moved in with me and Tailynn. Nicole was subletting her place until we found a house for all of us.

This morning, she'd left before giving me a kiss goodbye. She went to drop Tailynn off at school, since I had practice with the fellas. I was walking out of the penthouse to meet up with Marcus at the gym. As I walked down the steps and out of the building, I ran right into Genesis and Talbot, talking at the corner, as the swarm of paparazzi trailed behind.

I shook my head in annoyance. "Talbot, Genesis, what's up, guys?" I approached them and shook hands with them both.

"How you doing, Gage? I haven't seen you since the wedding. How does it feel to be a married man?" Genesis asked, grinning wickedly.

"Do they ever leave you alone? Or have a real job, besides following you around?" Talbot grunted at the crowd of paparazzi surrounding us.

"Are you forgetting your friend here is just as high profile as I am?" I answered, fiddling with my keys.

He waved me off as I slapped hands with them again, then walked to the driver's side door of my brand-new Dodge Charger that Nina had surprised me with for a wedding gift.

I pulled into the stadium, got out of the car, picked up my gym bag, and passed my keys to the valet and waved to the security personnel—Jamal and Luann. They'd both been here since I had joined the team. They were more like family than anyone at the stadium. A few fans stood outside, so I went back out to sign autographs and take pictures. Lately they've respected my boundaries, now that I'm married and her picture has been blasted all over the news. One thing I appreciate about her is that she is not letting the fame go to her head. Shaking hands with a few teammates, I headed through the double doors of the locker room. As usual, the music blasted with the latest track from Drake. Marcus was in the corner checking himself out in the mirror. Slapping him on the back, I stated, "Marcus, you're the only guy I know that stays in front of the mirror more than a woman." The entire room was filled with the team, and team doctors laughing at the veracity of my statement.

"Ladies love it, so it doesn't matter what you think."

"You say that now."

Placing my fresh jersey on the hanger, I removed my helmet from my bag and placed it on top of the shelf, along with my glove. I sat down on the bench, removed my shoes, and changed into my cleats.

"Today should just be a light workout, and then we have a meeting that the coach wanted to have to close out the season."

"Yeah, the email said we'd just get a check-up with the doctor and then run a few laps on the field. Shouldn't take up too much time, because I have plans with baby-doll later."

"Damn, you really are a married man now. I've never seen you ready to get home so fast to a woman."

"All it takes is the right one."

* * *

Nina

Hanging up the phone I finished going over what I already knew and what was expected going into this next phase of my life, confirming with the doctor that I was almost three months pregnant. I just wanted to sleep and not do anything else. I could see now that this was going to be a long process if all I wanted to do was eat and sleep. My body was athletic, and I barely wanted to go to the gym anymore.

After dropping Tailynn at school today, I called the girls up to meet me for lunch. Gage was off at baseball practice, according to the alert from TMZ, and Diya had mentioned the burger joint next to Talbot's tattoo shop. Stepping into the restaurant, I saw Maya sitting in the back corner with Diya and Nicole. It wasn't too crowded, so we had a little privacy. Hugging the ladies, I took a seat next to Nicole.

Diya passed me a menu just as the waitress came to our table. "Hi, I'm Lynette, I'll be your waitress today. Can I start you all with something to drink?" Lynette asked.

"We're ready to order, Lynette, I'll have the usual burger and fries," Diya declared handing off her menu.

"I'll take the kale salad, and a side of fries, along with a lemonade," Maya explained.

I gazed through the menu looking at the specials, and soup was the only thing I could really keep down these days. "Can I get the vegetable soup and crackers please, and a ginger ale," I said, watching Nicole looking lost in her phone.

"Nicole, what are you getting?" Maya poked Nicole in the arm.

She smacked her hand, scowled at her for trying to glance at who she was texting back and forth with. "Nothing, I'm not really hungry. So, NiNi, how's married life treating you?" Nicole cajoled, winking. Maya and Diya giggled at my expense. I had told all of them about the pregnancy after I had a talk with Scottie, and already they've planned out the baby shower.

"When are you planning on telling him you're pregnant?" Maya coaxed passing the menu to Lynette.

"Things are wonderful. We're looking at houses. Plus, Tailynn is doing great in school. Samantha just announced that she's pregnant. So now, I just need to tell Gage about our little unexpected surprise," I explained, rubbing my nonexistent belly.

"Cook dinner and seduce him," Maya suggested.

"The problem is, can I stay awake long enough to even try and seduce him, let alone cook dinner?"

"From the looks of things your condition is obviously evidence that your little seduction has worked in the past, because you're knocked up now."

"You're married to the richest man in sports; I think you can handle ordering from Uber Eats and lighting some candles," Nicole teased, cackling as I narrowed my eyes at her in a grimace.

* * *

A week later, the sun was bright and shining with cars lined up on the street of the community center. We even had the block cordoned off from oncoming traffic, thanks to a permit granted by the city. Having a husband that's well connected was beneficial for some things. My parents were throwing a party at the community center as a rebranding of the center—which was now appropriately named the Mitchell-Young Community Center. His family, along with our friends, all came together to celebrate our joint venture. The entire neighborhood came out to show us love. This was just the first of two locations that we'd opened as a collaboration with his new nonprofit foundation that he started. His family made a significant donation and decided to partner with other corporations to open more across the country. I knew deep down that it was simply a tax write off for his father, and a way of staying in his son's life after the debacle of trying to put my family's business out on the street. I was overseeing the day-to-day operations part time for him at the foundation, plus still working at the community center and tending to my duties as a mom-boss and wife, at least until we get a full-time leader. I was also using the occasion as a surprise announcement of the pregnancy, which I hadn't mentioned to my parents yet. Gage was so excited, and couldn't wait to show off to the world the fact that we were expecting.

Thinking back on the morning we ate breakfast together and surprised him after a long night of him keeping me up at night.

"Good morning, babe." Gage snuggled up behind me, wrapping his arms around my waist.

"Sit down breakfast is almost ready." I flipped the pancake around in the pan. Gage reached over to pick up a piece of bacon and I slapped him with the spatula.

"I'm hungry."

"You're always hungry." I frowned.

He grinned wiggling his brow. "Maybe you can help me from starving." Gage leaned forward, pecking me on the lips.

"No, Tailynn is up."

"Fine, leave your man hungry."

"Stop pouting and sit down," I nudged him away.

"Alright."

I turned the stove off, filling their plates up with food then left the kitchen and placed in front of him.

"Aren't you going to eat?" He lifted the fork and knife.

"I am, go ahead."

He cut into his pancake and I reached behind the chair to grab the bag and passed it to him, while he ate.

"Here, open this."

"It's not my birthday." He took it out of my hand, removing the gift box. "I know, it's even better."

Removing the bag, he flipped the box over opening it

up with a perplexed look on his face. "Babe a teddy bear dressed in my team uniform?"

"Read the inception."

Turning it around, his eyes drew tight focused, when all of a sudden they ballooned into a wide smile.

"We're pregnant, get ready for more players on the team," Gage read the print I had made at the Build-A-Bear.

"Surprise, I'm pregnant!"

Gage jumped up and pulled me into his arms, smothering me in kisses. "I love you."

"I love you, Gage."

"You're having my baby."

"I am."

"So, all that practice worked out."

"See, you're too much." I giggled as he walked us out of the kitchen and back to the bedroom.

Balloons hung on the perch of each pole with a large sign across the tents of our name and new logo of kids playing softball. Tailynn and Celine, two of the kids portrayed, looked like the next generation of female softball players, the generation that could lead the way of getting us equal pay and endorsements.

I walked up to the DJ stand and Gage stood beside me wearing a t-shirt like mine with our logo emblazoned across the front.

"Where's Li'l Bit?" I whispered to Gage to find Tailynn. He glanced around the field and spotted her jumping up and down in the Jumpzone machine with the other kids. Our friends were over in the corner talking to Maya. And Diya and Talbot were passing out gift bags.

"The Jumpzone machine kidnapped our child, we might as well announce now before everyone gets too far gone. I see your grandmother sitting down at a card table with Genesis, grandmother, MeMe, and it looks like she's teaching her how to gamble."

I observed what he was mentioning and I saw MeMe and my grandmother high-fiving each other, and Nicholas and my grandfather looking on with somber eyes at losing the pot of money they shouldn't be gambling with in the first place. She knew this was a function for the kids. I swear that old woman was crazy. I tapped the mic to get everyone's attention. "Can I have everyone's attention please? Granny, put the twenty back down and focus," I stated, shaking my head wryly.

Gage wrapped his arms around me, snuggling up against me.

"We are here today to celebrate the relaunch of our community center with the help of some very special people. I want to thank Gage and his family for continuing the movement of putting our kids first, and helping them to expand their education and journey in life with the programs they've brought to the center in areas ranging from STEM, coding, and filmmaking. "

He kissed the side of my cheek. I blushed and everyone clapped in celebration. "Not only are you here to celebrate this, but we also have a special announcement we'd like to share."

"I'm going to be a dad...again!" Gage yelled, and the crowd erupted in excitement and ran toward us as the banner was pulled down to show a 'We're Pregnant' sign as Tailynn came running toward him.

"I thought we agreed to let me tell everyone?" I pouted with my hands on both hips.

"Baby, you are too slow," he said with a grin, pecking my lips and bending down to pick up Tailynn.

"No, you're too fast."

"Wanna bet?" he suggested with a wink.

"No!" all our family and friends shouted at the same time. I rubbed my temples as Gage came to pull me into a kiss.

This was my future and I had no one to blame but myself, especially for taking him up on that first bet. I chuckled along with everyone as we continued to celebrate and enjoyed the festivities.

Epilogue

Gage

One year later...

We moved into a new, secluded house outside of the city. After all the craziness with the media, and my family trying to take over her family's business, I wanted a place that was our own. It was a hundred acres of prime land, with a six-car garage, an open deck with a pool, and a guesthouse. My dream to have a field in the backyard and one day raise my own kids to play baseball had come true. Our privacy was important to me, now that our family had expanded. Security was around the clock and included cameras and a gate on every side of the grounds. The mansion was three stories tall with a large archway and a long spiral staircase on both sides of the front entrance. Nina's office was on the first floor next to the playroom. She had decorated the entire place by herself and made sure to build me a man cave that I could sneak off to when I needed a break. The only help we had hired was my longtime nanny, Mrs. Harriet. Now that I was retired, I was thrilled with being a stay-at-home dad and a PTA leader.

I was watching Nina decorate the babies' playroom with Tailynn. We wanted to stick with the T names, so we decided to go with Taylor for a boy, and Thalia for a girl. They were six and a half months old now and were the most vibrant babies I'd ever seen.

"Daddy, can I get a cell phone? I'm a teenager now," Tailynn asked, sticking the photo of our wedding on the wall. She was nine now and seeing her blossom into a beautiful young woman was going to be hard on me. I wasn't prepared to see her go out on dates—she wasn't going to be allowed to date until she was fifty.

"Li'l Bit, you're too young for a cell phone. Besides, who do you need to talk to, other than your momma and me?" I questioned, helping lift her up to reach the top of the wall, so she could stick more pregnancy photos to it.

The babies stayed in the playpen, smiling and giggling. My heart swelled at seeing my family blossoming. "Babydoll, I want another baby—at least three more," I hinted, placing Tailynn back down on the floor. I moved closer to Nina, wrapped my arms around her waist, moved her hair to the side, and kissed the nape of her neck. She was still a little self-conscious about her weight gain from the twins, but I'd made it a family thing to keep her in the right mindset and let her know how beautiful she looked both on the inside and out. We all ate healthy and worked out together, Tailynn joined her in dance class, and the twins did Baby & Me classes with her on the weekends.

"Gage, you've lost your mind. The door is closed. We have three kids, and I'm working at the center, plus coaching softball on the weekends," Nina said, annoyed and panicked as she turned around in my arms, trying to push me away.

I sweetly kissed the tip of her nose. Her eyelids fluttered; she crossed her arms and pouted.

Chuckling, I ran a hand up across her back down to her plump ass that grew even bigger from having our babies. I squeezed, tapping her to follow me out of the room.

"Let me talk to you for a minute," I said in an effort to clear her head. Bending down, I scooped her up, cradling her like a bride as I started to carry her out of the nursery. "Li'l Bit, watch your brother and sister for a minute."

"Gage, put me down! Oh, my God, if you drop me, I swear!" Nina screamed, squirming in my arms, and trying to jump down. A flush of embarrassment grazed my face.

"Daddy, put Momma Nina down," Tailynn said, laughing and tickling Thalia as she giggled, almost dropping her pacifier. Tailynn picked it up from where it landed on her Wonder Woman onesie before it hit the floor and placed it back in her mouth.

Before Nina could get any words out to agree with Tailynn, I covered her mouth with a kiss and walked out of the room. Striding to our bedroom, I pushed the door open and closed it with my right foot. I placed her down on the bed, gently covering her entire body with mine.

Moving her braids out of her face, I kissed her cheek once, then twice. She tried covering her face away from me.

"This won't work."

"What won't work?" I questioned, resting my hands on both sides of her face.

"This! You charming your way into getting me to agree to have more babies. Gage, I love you, and I love our kids more than anything, but you have super-sperm, and I can't handle more kids. Finding out we were expecting twins was a shock, and who knows? If we try again, I might end up with triplets."

A smile touched the corners of my mouth. I bent down to kiss her deeply on the lips; our tongues danced their usual tango, and her fingers traced along the hard edges of my jawline. I pulled back to give us space before we could go further—especially with the kids still awake. We both knew that I could go for hours with no breaks.

"Babydoll, don't stress. We'll go at your own pace. If it happens, it happens. But I can't imagine not having more babies running around here, looking like you."

"So, you'll start wearing condoms?"

"Girl, the moment I went deep in your walls raw, my dick became allergic to condoms."

"Okay, so, a vasectomy?" she suggested, patting my cheek.

"Baby, you might as well divorce me now. Ain't no way in hell I'm getting a vasectomy," I chuckled, standing up and pulling her out of bed with me.

She stepped around me, heading to the door. "Okay, I'll check and see if that sexy player from the Atlanta Braves is seeing anyone," Nina teased, looking over her shoulder. She got the door halfway open before I shut it, grasping her in my arms. "Ahhhh! Gage, wait! I was kidding, baby!" Nina laughed, wrapping her legs around my waist.

"I don't share—and if you think any man will ever love you as much as I do, you're crazy. Especially a Braves player. Now, let's go back and finish putting the rest of the photos away in the nursery," I growled, gently biting the curve of her neck.

We both laughed, going back to the nursery, and

standing at the door, watching Tailynn play with her baby brother and sister.

From the moment we met, I knew that my life would change for the better having her in my life. After taking Talbot's advice to open my heart and not focus only on the game that I love, I was able to see that fulfillment would come in many forms if I only allowed myself to evolve into what I was meant to be. I was meant to be more than just Gage *'Billionaire Catcher'* Young. I was meant to be a husband, a father, a son, and a brother. Realizing all that finally realigned my beliefs.

* * *

I hope you enjoyed **Gage** and **Nina**, if you want to see more of these character check out bonus scenes here "https://chiquitadennie.squarespace.com/bonus-scenes , Ethan and Maya has a story to tell in **Bossy Billionaire** here "https://books2read.com/u/4E8JLg

Follow TN Seal Security series with a standalone, opposites attract, fake dating, military romance "**Nicco**" https://books2read.com/u/4DDn7k Are you a fan of sports romance? Then download one-night stand, billionaire romance "**Refuel**" https://books2read.com/u/b6Gaop Also, follow it up with workplace, sports romance "**Pressure**"https://books2read.com/u/bPeDqr If you love romantic comedy, fake relationships, enemies to lovers, find it here, "**Something Gained.**" Click the link here https://books2read.com/u/baGLYy. My stories of friends finding love started with the Heart of Stone series that includes a host of characters and family. "**Broken**" book 1 Emery and Jackson a sports, one night stand, workplace romance is here: https://books2read.com/u/3LoelX

Then you can continue with a fun side story of Emery and Jackson with "Valentine's Day short here: https://books2read.com/u/4jAypY

Jordan, her best friend's story, continues here in **"Rebirth"** book 2 a single dad, widow billionaire romance here: https://books2read.com/u/ba2OMx If you love bonus content click here "https://chiquitadennie.squarespace.com/bonus-scenes

* * *

Please also check out a second-chance workplace romance here, **"Renew Book 4"** https://books2read.com/u/4NXyPG with a host of characters intertwined.

Follow Desiree and Gabriel in **"Temptation"** a standalone contemporary, sports, curvy girl romance. Check it out here https://books2read.com/u/mle1Vv

Check out dark mafia romance here that started my journey with Antonio and Sabrina in **"Ruthless Book 1"** https://books2read.com/u/4AxKLo

The relationship continues in **"Savage"** book 2 as they get to know each other and their families: https://books2read.com/u/bpED6g

Antonio and Sabrina have more work to do in **"Beast"** book 3 right here: https://books2read.com/links/ubl/4AxKOd

* * *

Did you know Janice and Carlo have a book? Well

grab this dark mafia romance with emotional scars, and betrayal right here: https://books2read.com/u/b6je6M

Any fans of forbidden romance, political? Check out "**Mutual Agreement**" https://books2read.com/u/mgzzWX a steamy romance. Do you love workplace romantic suspense? Then check out "**Aydin**" https://books2read.com/u/mBwaOy and the interconnected standalone hate to love, actress, damsel in distress bodyguard romance "**Nasir**" click the link here https://books2read.com/u/3Ln7Ee

Have you checked out "**She's All I Need**" click here https://books2read.com/u/49lkeW a sports, opposites attract romance. What about dark romance that has everything from steamy romance, opposites attract, suspense, thriller, celebrity, and more "**Stolen Book 1**" https://books2read.com/u/mvZlgV Don't miss the follow up Joaquin and Sofia's story in book 2 "**Saved**" https://books2read.com/u/4DWwLd

The conclusion for Joaquin and Sofia comes full circle in "**Betrayed**" here: https://books2read.com/u/4A5LGp

* * *

Catch up with favorite characters in this holiday short romance which includes spoilers. "**Holiday collection**" here https://books2read.com/u/bzd59G

For small town, single mom stories check out "**Until Seren**a" https://books2read.com/u/mej8vr. Always fun when you love billionaire romances so check in with "**Cocky Catcher**" a sports romance, enemies to lovers here:https://books2read.com/u/3nGX55

Some familiar characters show up in "**Bossy Billionaire**" a workplace, enemies to lovers romance here:https://books2read.com/u/4E8JLg

All curvy girl, plus size romance lovers get into "**I Deserve His Love**" a standalone, second chance romance here: https://books2read.com/u/mVrGwP

The fantasy romance readers look no further than a "**Red Light District**" a curvy girl, fling romance here: https://books2read.com/u/m2RQ6G

Spotify Playlist

1. Cocky—A$Ap Rocky, Gucci Mane, 21 Savage
2. I Get the Bag—Gucci Mane
3. Glamorous—Fergie, Ludacris
4. Summer—The Carters
5. Waves—Normani, 6Lack
6. Peaches and Cream—112
7. Can't Take My Eyes Off You—Lauryn Hill
8. Just Friends—Musiq Soulchild
9. Say Yes—Floetry
10. My Love—Justin Timberlake, TI
11. Miss Independent—NeYo
12. Suit & Tie—Justin Timberlake

Acknowledgments

A huge thank you to my team that helps me behind the scenes, from my editors, test readers, graphic designers, and the list goes on. Truly appreciate each of you for keeping me on my toes.

Heart of Stone Universe

Broken 1 Emery and Jackson
https://books2read.com/u/boWPAV
Heart of Stone Book 1.5
https://payhip.com/b/kWg7
Rebirth 2 Jordan and Damon
https://books2read.com/u/ba2OMx
Heart of Stone Book 3.5 Bottoms Up
https://payhip.com/b/HGP1
Reveal 3 Angela and Brent
https://books2read.com/u/31rx9l
Renew 4 Jessica and Joseph
https://books2read.com/u/4NXyPG

Struck In Love Universe

The Early Years-A Prequel
https://books2read.com/u/49Zjnw
Ruthless Struck In Love Book 1
https://books2read.com/u/4AxKLo
Savage Struck In Love Book 2
https://books2read.com/u/bpED6g
Beast Struck In Love Book 3
https://books2read.com/u/3LpgdJ
Janice and Carlo Captivated By His Love
https://books2read.com/u/b6je6M
Brutal Struck In Love Book 4
https://books2read.com/u/4NQyE9
Stolen-Fuertes Mafia Cartel Book 1
https://books2read.com/u/mvZlgV
Saved-Fuertes Mafia Cartel Book 2
https://books2read.com/u/4DWwLd
Redemption Struck In Love Book 5
https://books2read.com/u/b5kZ8O
Betrayal- Fuertes Mafia Cartel Book 3
https://books2read.com/u/4A5LGp

Also By Chiquita Dennie

Series

<u>Struck in Love</u>

The Early Years-A Prequel Short Story
Ruthless:Antonio and Sabrina Book 1
Savage: Antonio and Sabrina Book 2
Beastl: Antonio and Sabrina Book 3
Captivated By His Love:Janice and Carlo
Brutal: Antonio and Sabrina Booke 4
Redemption: Antonio and Sabrina Book 5

<u>Heart of Stone</u>

Broken, Book 1 (Emery & Jackson)
A Valentine's Day Short Book 1.5 Emery & Jackson
Rebirth, Book 2 (Jordan and Damon)
Reveal, Book 3 (Angela and Brent)
Bottoms Up Book 3.5 Jessica and Joseph Short
Renew, Book 4 (Jessica and Joseph)

<u>Cocky Billionaire Boys</u>

Cocky Catcher (Cocky Billionaire Boys Book 1)
Bossy Billionaire (Cocky Billionaire Boys Book 2)

The Fuertes Cartel

Stolen (The Fuertes Cartel Book 1)
Saved (The Fuertes Cartel Book 2)
Betrayed (The Fuertes Cartel Book 3)

Carrington Cartel

Torn: The Carrington Cartel Book 1
Claim: The Carrington Cartel Book 2

Something

Something Gained: A Romantic Comedy Book 1
Something Earned: A Romantic Comedy Book 2

Pierce Motors

Refuel:(Pierce Motors Book 1)
Pressure:(Pierce Motors Book 2)

Summer Break

Summer Nights(Summer Break Book 1)

TN Seal Security

Aydin: Book 1
Nasir: Book 2
Nicco: Book 3

Standalones

Until Serena(HEA World Novel)
Temptation
She's All I Need

I Deserve His Love
Mutual Agreement
Scoring with Sadie
Exposed (A Bodyguard Novel)
Love Shorts:A Collection of Short Stories
Red Light District(A Fantasy Romance Short)

<u>By Keke Renée:</u>
Wet Heat
His Peace, Her Pleasure
Baby, It's Cold Outside
Love Don't Live Here Anymore, Book 1, 2
Every Time We Touch (A Wet Heat Novelette)
One Night Only- Love By Design Book 1
Cassian and Savannah Love By Design Book 2
Deidra's Love -Love By Design Book 3
Protecting Bria: Book 1
Protecting Chanel:Book 2
Protecting Yanira: Book 3
Haven: A Single Dad Romance
Sensual
Seek to Please: Book 1
Seek To Touch: Book 2
Seek To Bare:Book 3
Seek To Love: Book 4
Seek To Trust: Book 5
Seek To Earn: Book 6
Tease Me: Book 1
Promise Me: Book 1

<u>By Ava S.King</u>
Fatal Memory: Book 1 Teagan Stone
Fatal Target: Book 2 Teagan Stone

Fatal Crime: Book 3 Teagan Stone
Fatal Justice: Book 4 Teagan Stone
Fatal Enemy: Book 5 Teagan Stone
Fatal Death: Book 6 Teagan Stone
Fatal Revenge: Book 7 Teagan Stone
Fatal Pursuit: Book 8 Teagan Stone
Mirror of Lies: Book 1
Mirror of Lust: Book 2
Ruined: Andi Easton Book 1
Thank you so much for reading and if you enjoyed the crazy ride and decide to leave a review we'd truly appreciate the support..

About the Author

Chiquita Dennie is an author of Contemporary, Romantic Suspense, Erotic, and Women's Fiction.

Chiquita lives in Los Angeles, CA. Before she started writing contemporary romance, she worked in the entertainment industry on notable TV shows such as the Dr. Phil show, the Tyra Banks show, American Idol, and Deal or No Deal. But her favorite job is the one she's now doing: full-time writing romance.

A best-selling author and award-winning filmmaker, her first short film, "Invisible," was released in summer 2017 and screened in multiple festivals and won for Best Short Film. She also hosts a podcast that showcases the latest in beauty, business, and community called "Moscato and Tea." Her debut release of *Antonio and Sabrina Struck in Love* has opened a new avenue of writing that she loves. Nominated for 2021 Author of the Year, Best Black Romance "Mutual Agreement," and Best Interracial Romance for "She's All In Need". In 2022 nominated Author Queen of the Year, Best Black Romance "Nasir" Best Interracial Romance "Torn" and Best Romantic Comedy "Something Gained" by Black Girls Who Write.

If you want to know when the next book will come out, please visit my website at http://www.chiquitadennie.com, where you can sign up to receive an email for my next release.

What's Next?

Want to know what happens next?

Follow me on social media to catch the next release.

Reviews are the lifeblood of the publishing world. They're read, appreciated, and needed. Please consider taking the time to leave a few words on Goodreads, or bookbub.

Sign up for updates and sneak peaks at the site below.
https://www.bookbub.com/chiquitadennie
https://www.chiquitadennie.com
https://www.goodreads.com/author/chiquitadennie
https://Facebook.com/chiquitassteamyreadinggroup
x.com/authorchiquitad
https://www.instagram.com/authorchiquitadennie
https://www.Facebook.com/authorchiquitadennie
https://www.304publishing.tumblr.com

304 Publishing Company

We showcase authors writing Romance, Women's Fiction, Thriller, and Erotic.Along with Mystery, Suspense, Poetry, Beauty, and Style Books. Thank you for taking the time out to visit. Join our mailing list to stay updated with new releases and blog posts.